1   1236

795
6.95

jacket
front

THE HOTEL EDEN

Betrayed by F. Scott Fitzgerald
A Novel

Truants
A Novel

The News of the World
Stories

Plan B for the Middle Class
Stories

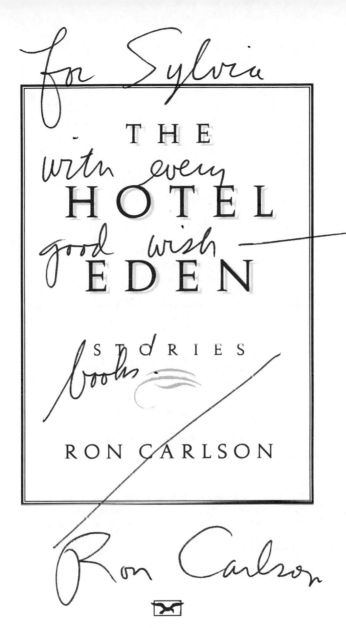

THE
HOTEL
EDEN

STORIES

RON CARLSON

For Sylvia —
with every
good wish —
books:

Ron Carlson

W. W. NORTON & COMPANY
NEW YORK · LONDON

For information about permission to reproduce selections from this book,
write to Permissions, W. W. Norton & Company, Inc., 500 Fifth Avenue,
New York, NY 10110.

The text of this book is composed in Granjon
with the display set in Nova Augustea
Composition by Crane Typesetting Service, Inc.
Manufacturing by Vail Ballou Press
Book design by JAM Design

Library of Congress Cataloging-in-Publication Data

Carlson, Ron.
    The Hotel Eden, stories / Ron Carlson.
        p.   cm.
    Contents: The Hotel Eden—Keith—The prisoner of Bluestone—
Zanduce at second—The house goes up—What we wanted to do—
note on the type—The chromium hook—Nightcap—Dr. Slime—
Down the green river—Oxygen.
    ISBN 0-393-04068-2
    I. Title
PS3553.A733H68   1997
813'.54—dc20   96-42425
                                                                        CIP

W. W. Norton & Company, Inc., 500 Fifth Avenue, New York, N.Y. 10110
http://www.wwnorton.com

W. W. Norton & Company Ltd., 10 Coptic Street, London WC1A 1PU

1 2 3 4 5 6 7 8 9 0

for Walter DeMelle

CONTENTS

ACKNOWLEDGMENTS

SOME OF THE stories in this collection appeared, sometimes in slightly different form, in the following publications: *Double-Take*: "Nightcap"; *Esquire*: "The Hotel Eden"; *Harper's*: "Zanduce at Second," "A Note on the Type," "What We Wanted to Do," "The Chromium Hook"; *Gentlemen's Quarterly*: "The Prisoner of Bluestone"; *Salt Lake City Magazine*: "Nightcap"; *The Southern Review*: "Down the Green River"; *Tell*: "Keith"; *Western Humanities Review*: "Dr. Slime"; *Witness*: "What We Wanted to Do," "Oxygen."

Special thanks to the editors of these publications, particularly Colin Harrison, Ben Metcalf, Tom Mallon, and Dave Smith.

"Keith" also appeared in the anthology *Success Stories of the Nineties*; and "A Note on the Type" was published as a letter-press book from Mile Wide Press (Penland, North Carolina) in an edition of one hundred copies, each with a cover of galvanized roof flashing and type hand-set by the determined Eileen Wallace, 1996. "A Note on the Type" also appeared in *The Writ-*

ing Path 2, edited by Michael Pettit, University of Iowa Press, 1996.

I would also like to express my gratitude to Gail Hochman for constant and everlasting faith; Marianne Merola for her encouragement; to Ed Dee for the Jack Frost line; to Bill Mai for kindnesses in the Old World; to Christopher Merrill for his enthusiasms; to David Kranes for friendship and astute reading; to Michael Phillips for help in the snow; to Carol Houck Smith for tenacity and grace; to Ashley Barnes for her smart efforts on my behalf; and to Elaine and Nick and Colin for all these delicious years and those to come.

I

Let me make this kind of mistake with you,

let me tell you everything.

THE HOTEL EDEN

THAT YEAR THE place we would go after hours was the Hotel
Eden. It had a cozy little bar in the parlor with three tiny tables
and four stools at the counter. You had to walk sideways to get
around, and it had a low ceiling and thick old carpets, but it had
a roomy feeling and it became absolutely grand when Porter was
there. Over the course of the spring he told us a hundred stories
in the Eden and changed things for us.

The barman was a young Scot named Norris who seemed
neither glad nor annoyed when we'd come in around midnight
after closing down one of the pubs, the Black Swan or the Lamb
and Flag or the forty others we saw that cold spring. Pub hours
then were eleven o'clock last call, and drink up by eleven-fifteen.
Porter would set his empty pint glass on the whatever bar and
say to Allison and me, "The Eden then?" He'd bike over, regardless of where we were, out on the Isle of Dogs or up in
Hampstead, and Allison would get us a cab.

Norris would have the little curtain pulled down above the

bar, a translucent yellow sheet that said, "Residents Only." He drew it down every night at eleven; hotels could serve late to their guests. Porter had done some favor for the manager of the Hotel Eden when he'd come to London years before, and he had privileges. They became in a sense our privileges too, though— as you shall see—I was only in the Eden alone on one occasion. The curtain just touched your forehead if you sat at the bar.

We often arrived ahead of Porter, and Norris would set us up with pints of lager, saying always, "Hello, miss," when he placed Allison's glass. The Eden didn't have bitter. I remember the room as always being empty when we'd arrive, and it was a bit of a mystery at first as to why Norris was still even open. But there were times when there was a guest or two, a man or a man and a woman, having a brandy at one of the tables. We were quiet too, talking about Allison's research at the museum—she had a year in London to work on her doctorate in Art History. But it was all airy, because we were really just waiting for Porter. It was as if we weren't substantial enough to hold down our stools, and then Porter would come in, packing his riding gloves into his helmet, running a hand through his thick black hair, saying, "Right enough, Norris, let's commence then, you gloomy Northlander," and gravity would be restored. His magnetism was tangible, and we'd wait for him to speak. When he had the pint of lager in his hand, he'd turn to Allison and say something that would start the rest of the night.

One night, he lifted his glass and said, "Found a body today." Then he drank.

Allison leaned in: "A dead man?"

"Dead as Keats and naked as Byron." We waited for him to go on. His was the voice of experience, the world, the things that year that I wanted so much.

"Where?" I asked.

"Under the terrace at the Pilot."

"The place on the river?" Allison asked. He'd taken us walking through the Isle of Dogs after we'd first met and we'd stopped at half a dozen pubs which backed onto the Thames.

"Right, lady. Spoiled my lunch, he did, floating under there like that."

Allison was lit by this news. We both were. And there it was: the night kicked in at any hour, no matter how late. When Porter arrived, things *commenced*. We both leaned closer. Porter, though he'd just sucked the top off his pint, called Norris for another, and the evening was launched.

We always stayed until Porter leaned back and said, "It's a night then." He didn't have an accent to us, being American, but he had the idiom and he had the way of putting his whole hand around a glass and of speaking over the top of a pint with the smallest line of froth of his upper lip, something manly really, something you'd never correct or try to touch off him, that was something to us I can only describe as being *real*. He'd been at Hilman College years before Allison and me, and he knew Professor Mills and all the old staff and he'd even been there the night of the Lake Dorm Fire, the most famous thing about Hilman really, next to Professor Mills, I suppose. I spent a hundred hours with him in the Eden that spring, like Allison, twelve inches across that little round table or huddled as we were at the bar, and I memorized Porter really, his face, the smooth tan of red veins running up under his eyes, as if he'd stood too close to some special fire, and his white teeth, which he showed you it seemed for a purpose. His nose had been broken years ago. We played did you know so-and-so until Allison, who was still a member of Lake Sorority, brought up the fire.

"Oh yes," he said. "I was there. What's the legend grown to now? A hundred ghosts?"

"Six," Allison laughed. "There's always been six."

"Always," he protested. "You make it sound ancient. Hey, I was there. February." Then he added with authority and precision: "Fifteen years ago."

"Someone had stopped the doors with something; the six girls couldn't get out."

Porter drew on his beer and looked at me. "Hockey sticks. It was a bundle of hockey sticks through the door handles."

"That's right."

"Oh." He looked from me to Allison. "It was awful. A cold night at Hilman, and you know, it could get cold, ten degrees, old snow on the ground hard as plastic, and the colossal inferno. From the quad you could see the trapped figures bumping into the glass doors. A group of us came up from town, the Villager had just closed, you ever drink there?"

"It's now a cappuccino place," Allison said. "The Blue Dish."

"Ah, the old Villager was a capital dive. That bar could tell some tales. It's where I met our Professor Mills. Anyway, they closed at one, and when I stepped out into the winter night, there was this ethereal light pulsing from the campus like a heartbeat, and you had to go. There was no choice. I knew right away it was Lake, fully engaged, as they say, a fire like no other, trying to tear a hole in the world." Allison and I were mesmerized, and he finished: "It singed the sycamores back to Dobbs Street, and that's where a group of us stood. It hurt to look. In the explosive light, I could see figures come to the glass, they looked like fish."

When he'd finish talking like that, telling this story or that— he'd found a downed ultralight plane in the Cotswolds once on a walking tour and had had to secure the pilot's compound leg fracture—Allison and I would be unable to move. It was a spell. It's that simple. You see, we were graduate students and we weren't used to this type of thing. I'd tell you what we were used to but it all seems to drop out of memory like the bottom of a wet cardboard box. We were used to nothing: to weeks at the library at Hilman in Wisconsin and then some vacation road trips with nothing but forced high jinx and a beach. There was always one of our friends, my roommate or Allison's roommate, who would either read Dylan Thomas aloud all the way to Florida and then refuse to leave the car or get absolutely drunk for a week and try to show everyone his or her genitals as part of a discussion of our place in the universe. We were Americans and we knew it. I was twenty-three and Allison was twenty-four. We hadn't done anything, we were scholars. I'd finished my master's degree in meteorology at Northern near Hilman and was doing what—nothing. Allison got her grant. Going to England was a big deal for us. She was going to do her research at the British Museum. I was going to cool out and do London. Then we met Porter.

Allison's mentor at Hilman, the famous Professor Julie Mills, had given us some telephone numbers, and after we found a flat in Hampstead and after Allison had established a routine with her work, we called the first guy. His name was Roger Ardreprice, the assistant curator of Keats's House, and he had us meet him over there as things were closing up one cold March night. He was a smug little guy who gave us his card right away and walked with both hands in his jacket pockets and finished all his sentences with "well um um." We walked over to the High Street and then down to the Pearl of India with him talking about Professor Mills, whom he called Julie. Evidently he'd met other of her students in former years, and he assumed his role as host of all of London with a kind of jaded enthusiasm; it was clear he'd seen our kind before. It was at the long dinner that we met two other people who had studied at Hilman with the famous Professor Julie Mills. One was a quiet well-dressed woman named Sarah Garrison who worked at the Tate, and the other was a thirtyish man in a green windbreaker who came late, said hello, and then ate in the back at a table by the kitchen door with two turbaned men who evidently were the chefs. This was Porter.

Of course, we didn't talk to him until afterward. Roger Ardreprice ran a long dinner which was half reverential shop-talk about Julie Mills and half sage advice about life in London, primarily about things to avoid. Roger had a practiced world-weary smile which he played all night, even condescending to Sarah Garrison, who seemed to me to be a real nice woman. It was a relief when we finally adjourned sometime after eleven and stepped from the close spicy room onto the cold sidewalk. Sarah took a cab and Roger headed down for his tube stop, and so Allison and I had the walk up the hill. I remember the night well, the penetrating cold wind, our steps past all the shops we would eventually memorize: the newsdealer, the kabob stand, the cheese shop, the Rosslyn Arms. We were a week in London and the glow was very much on everything, even a chilly night after a strange dinner. Then like a phantom, a figure came suddenly from behind us and banked against the curb, a man on a bicycle. He pulled the goggles off his head and said, "Enough curry with Captain Prig then?" He grinned the most beguiling grin, the corners of his mouth puckered. "Want a pint?"

"It's after hours," I said.

"This is the most interesting city in the world," he said. "Certainly we can find a pint." He stopped a cab and spoke to the driver and herded us inside, saying, "See you in nineteen minutes."

And so we were delivered to the Hotel Eden. That first night we waited in front on the four long white stone steps until we saw him turn onto the street, all business on his bicycle, nineteen minutes later. "Yes, indeed," he said, dismounting and taking a deep breath through his nose as if sensing something near. "The promise of lager. Which one of you studied with Julie Mills?"

Allison said, "I did. I do. I finish next year."

"Nice woman," he said as he pulled open the old glass door of the hotel. "I slept with her all my senior year." Then he turned to us as if apologizing. "But we were never in love. Let's have that straight."

I thought Allison was going to be sick after that news. Professor Mills was widely revered, a heroine, a goddess, certainly someone who would have a wing of the museum named after her someday. Then we went into the little room and met Norris and he drew three beautiful pints of lager, gold in glass, and set them before us.

"Why'd you eat with the cooks?" Allison asked Porter.

"That's the owner and his brother," Porter said. His face was ruddy in the half-light of the bar. "They're Sikhs. Do you know about the Sikhs?"

We shook our heads no.

"Don't mess with them. They're merciless. Literally. The man who sat at my right has killed three people."

I nodded at him, flattered that he thought I'd mess with anyone at all, let alone a bearded man in a turban.

"I'm doing a story on their code." Porter drank deeply from his glass. "Besides, your Mr. Roger Ardreprice, Esquire, has no surplus love for me." He smiled. "And you . . ." He turned his glorious smile to Allison, and reached out and took her shiny brown hair in his hand. "You're certainly a Lake. We'll have to get you a tortoiseshell clip for that Lake hair." Lake was the prime sorority at Hilman. "What brings you to London besides the footsteps of our Miss Mills?—who founded Lake, of course, a thousand years ago."

Allison talked a little about the Egyptian influence on the Victorians, but it was halfhearted, the way all academic talk is in a pub, and my little story about my degree in meteorology felt absolutely silly. I had nothing to say to this man, and I wanted something. I wanted to warn him about something with an exacting and savage code, but there was nothing. I wasn't going to say what I had said to my uncle at a graduation party, "I got good grades."

But Porter turned to me, and I can still feel it like a light, his attention, and he said, with a kind of respect, "The weather. Oh that's very fine. The weather," he turned to me and then back to Allison, "and art. That is absolutely formidable." He wasn't kidding. It was the first time in the seven months since I'd graduated that I felt I had studied something real, and the feeling was good. I felt our life in London assume a new dimension, and I called for another round.

That was the way we'd see him; he would turn up. We'd go four, five days with Allison working at the museum and me tramping London like a tourist, which I absolutely was, doing only a smattering of research, and then there'd be a one-pound note stapled to a page torn from the map book *London A to Z* in our mailbox with the name of a pub and an hour scribbled on it. The Flask, Highgate, 9 p.m., or Old Plover, on the river, 7. And we'd go. He would have seen the Prince at Trafalgar Square or stopped a fight in Hyde Park and there'd be a bandage across his nose to prove it. He was a character, and I realize now we'd never met one. I'd known some guys in the dorms who would do crazy things drunk on the weekend, but I'd never met anybody in my life who had done and seen so much. He was out in the world, and it all called to me.

He took us to the Irish pubs in Kilburn, all the lights on, everyone scared of a suitcase bomb, the men sitting against the wall in their black suits drinking Guinness. We went to three different pubs, all well lit and quiet, and Porter told us not to talk too loud or laugh too loud or do anything that might set off these powder kegs. "Although there's no real danger," he added, pointing at Allison's L. L. Bean boots. "They're not going to harm an American schoolgirl. And such a beautiful member of the Lake."

Maybe harm was part of the deal, the attraction, I know it probably was for me. I'd spend two days straight doing some of my feeble research, charting rainfall (London has exactly fifteen rain days per month, year-round), and then, with my shoulders cramping and my fingers stained with the wacky English marking pens we bought, I'd be at the Eden bent over a pint looking into Porter's fine face and it would all go away. He showed up early in March with his arm in a sling and a thrilling scrape across his left cheekbone. Someone had opened a car door on him as he'd biked home one night. The gravel tracks where he'd hit the road made a bright fan under his eye. His grin seemed magnified that night under our concern.

"Nothing," he said of it. "The worst is I can't ride for a week. It puts me in the tube with all the rest of you wankers." He laughed. "Say, Norris," he called. "Is there any beer in here?" I saw Allison's face, the worry there, and knew she was a goner. And I was a goner too. I'd never had a scratch on my body.

Porter was too much, and I knew that this is the way I did it, had crushes, and I'd fallen for two or three people before: Professor Cummins, my thesis chair, with his black bowl of hair and bright blue eyes, a cartoon face really, but he'd traveled the world and in his own words been rained on in ninety-nine countries; and Julie Mills, who worked so closely with Allison. I'd met her five or six times at receptions and such, and her intensity, the way she set her hand below my shoulder when speaking to me as if to steady me for the news to come, and the way there was a clear second between each of her words, these things printed themselves on me, and I tried them out with no success. I tried everything and had little success generating any conviction that I might find a personality for me.

And now Allison kidded me when we'd have tea somewhere or a plowman's platter in a pub: "You don't have to try Porter's frown when you ask for a pint," she'd say. "This isn't the Eden." And I'd taken certain idiomatic inflections from Porter's accent, and when they'd slip out, Allison would turn to me, alert to it. I would have stopped it if I could. I started being assertive and making predictions, the way Porter did. We'd gone to Southwark one night, and after a few at a dive called Old Tricks, we'd stood at the curb afterward, arm in arm in the chill, and he'd said, "Calm enough now," and he'd scanned the low apartment buildings on the square, "but this will all be in flames in two years. Put it in your calendar." And when I got that way with Allison, even making a categorical statement about being late for the tube or forgetting the umbrella, she'd say, "Put it in your calendar, mate." I always smiled at these times and tried to shrug them off. She was right, after all. But I also knew she'd fallen too. She didn't pick up the posture or the walk, but Allison was in love with this character too.

One night in March, he met us at the Eden with a plan. I was a meteorologist, wasn't I? It was key for a truly global understanding of the weather for me to visit the north Scottish coast and see the effects of the Gulf Stream firsthand. "Think of it, Mark," he said, his face lit by the glass of beer. "The Gulf Stream. All that water roiling against the coast of Mexico, warming in the equatorial sun, then spooling out around the corner of Florida and up across the Atlantic four thousand miles still warm as it pets the forehead of Scotland. It's absolutely tropical. Palm trees. We better get up there."

Well, I didn't have anything to do. I was on hold, taking a year off we called it sometimes, and I looked at Allison there in the Eden. She raised her eyebrows at me, throwing me the ball, and smiled. Her hair was back in the new brown clip Porter had given her. "Sounds too good to pass up," she said. "Mark's ready for an adventure."

"Capital," Porter said. "I'll arrange train tickets. We'll leave Wednesday."

Allison and I talked about it in our flat. It was chilly all the time, and we'd get in the bed sometimes in the early afternoon and talk and maybe have a snack, some cheese and bread with some Whitbred from a canister. She came home early from the museum the Tuesday before I was to leave with Porter. There was a troubled look on her face. She undressed and got in beside me. "Well," she said. "Ready for your adventure?" Her face was strange, serious and fragile, and she put her head into my shoulder and held me.

"Hey, don't worry," I said. The part of her sweet hair was against my mouth. "You've got the people at the museum if you need anything, and if something came up you could always call Roger Ardreprice." I patted the naked hollow of her back to let her know that I had been kidding with that last, but she didn't move. "Hey," I said, trying to sit up to look her in the eyes, comfort her, but she pushed me back, burrowed in.

PORTER AND I left London in the late afternoon and clacked through the industrial corridor of the city until just before the early dark the fields began to open and hedgerows grow farther apart. Porter had arrived late for the train and kicked his feet up on the opposite seat, saying, "Sorry, mate, but I've got the ticket right here." He withdrew a glass jar from his pack and examined it. "Not a leak. Tight and dry." He held the jar like a trophy and smiled at me his gorgeous smile. "Dry martinis, and we're going to get *very* tight." Then he unwrapped two white china coffee cups and handed me one. There was a little gold crown on each cup, the blue date in Roman numerals MCMLIII. He saw me examining the beautiful cup and said, "From the coronation. But there are no saucers and—in the finest tradition of the empire—no ice."

Well, I was thrilled. Here I was rambling north in a foreign country, every mile was farther north in Britain than I'd ever been, etc., and Porter was dropping a fat green olive in my cup and covering it with silver vodka. "This is real," I said aloud, and I felt satisfied at how it felt.

"To Norris," I said, making the first toast, "and the Eden, hoping they're happy tonight."

"Agreed," Porter said, drinking. "But happy's not the word, mate. Norris is pleased, but never happy. He's been a good friend to me, these English years."

"We love him," I said, speaking easily hearing the "we," Allison entering the sentence as a natural thing. It was true. We'd

often remarked as we'd caught the tube back to Hampstead or
as we'd headed toward the Eden that Norris was wonderful. In
fact he was one of eight people we knew by name in that great
world city.

"Allison seems a dear girl." Porter said. It was a strange thing,
like a violation, the two of us talking about her.

"She's great," I said, simply holding place.

"Women." Porter raised his cup. "The great unknowable."

I thought about Allison, missing her in a different way. We
were tender people, that is, *kids,* and our only separations had
been play ones, vacations when she'd go home to her folks and
I'd go home to my folks, and then we moved in together after
graduating with no fanfare, tenderly, a boy and a girl who were
smart and well-meaning. Our big adventure was going off to
England together, which everyone we knew and our families
thought was a wonderful idea, and who knows what anybody
meant by that, and really, who knows what we meant at such a
young age, what we were about. We were lovers, but that term
would have embarrassed us, and there are no other words which
come close to the way we were. We liked each other a lot, that's
it. We both knew it. We were waiting for something to happen,
something to do with age and the world that would tell us if we
were qualified, if we were in love, the real love. And here I was
on a train with a stranger, each mile sending me farther from
her into a dark night in a foreign country. I thought about her in
the quilts of our small bed in Hampstead. The first martini was
working, and it had made me large: I was a man on a train far
from home.

We got drunk. Porter grinned a lot and I actually made him
giggle a few times with my witty remarks. The vodka evidently

made me very clever. About nine o'clock we went up to the club car, a little snack bar, and bought some Scotch eggs. This was real life, I could feel it. I'd had a glimpse of it from time to time with Porter, but now here we were.

One long afternoon after we'd first met him, he took us on a walk through the Isle of Dogs. He'd had us meet him at the Bridge & Beacon near the foot of London Bridge and we'd spent the rest of the day tramping the industrial borough of the Isle. The pubs were hidden among all the fenced construction storage lots and warehouses. We'd walk a quarter mile down a street with steel sheeting on both sides and then down a little alley would be the entry to the Bowsprit or the Sea Lion or the Roman Arch, places that had been selling drinks for three hundred years while the roads outside, while everything outside, changed. They all had a dock and an entry off the Thames. For us it was enchanting, this lost world at once rough, crude, and romantic. Two steps down under a huge varnished beam into a long room of polished walnut and brass lamps, like the captain's quarters on a ship, we'd follow Porter and sit by the window where the river spread beneath us. He'd call the barman by name and order three pints. I mean, we loved this stuff. We were on the inside.

"Do you know the opening of *Heart of Darkness?*" he asked. We'd never read it. "Right here," he said, sweeping his hand at the window. "At anchor here on a sloop in the sea reach of the Thames." And then he'd pull the paperback from his pocket and read the first two pages. "Geez, that makes a man thirsty, eh, Mark?" He'd bump me and we'd drink up.

It was a long tour. We left the London Bridge sometime after five and didn't cross under the river in the tunnel at Greenwich until almost eleven. I remember scurrying through the long tiled corridor far beneath the river behind Porter as he dragged us along in a hurry because the pubs were going to close and we'd miss the last train back to Hampstead. We were all full of beer and Allison and I were dislocated, a feeling I got used to and came to like, as we came out into the bright cold air and saw the *Cutty Sark* moored there. This was life, it seemed to me, and I ran into the Red Cloak on Porter's footsteps. I was bursting and so pleased to be headed for the men's when he took my arm and pulled me to the bar. "Let's have a pint first, just to savor the night," he said. I wasn't standing upright, having walked with a bladder cramp for half a mile, and now the pain and pressure were blinding. I gripped the glass and met his smile. Allison came out of the ladies' and came over. "Are we being macho or just self-destructive?" she said.

"We're playing through the pain," Porter said. "We're seeing if the Buddhists are right with their wheel of desire and misery." I could barely hear him; there was a rushing in my ears, a cataract of steady noise. Disaster was imminent. Porter took a big slug of the bitter, and I mirrored his action. We swallowed and put down the glasses. "Excuse me," he said. "Think I'll hit the loo." And he strolled slowly into the men's. A blurred moment later I stood beside him at the huge urinals, dizzy and reclaimed. "We made it, mate," he said. "Now we've got to pound down a thousand beers and catch the train."

It had been a strange season in London for me. It was all new and as they say exciting, but I couldn't figure out what any of it meant. Now on the train to the north coast with Porter, I actually felt like somebody else who had never had my life, because as I saw it, my life—high school, college, Allison—hadn't taught me anything. For the first time I didn't give a shit about what happened next. The little play dance of cause and effect, be a good student, was all gone.

"You're not married," I said. It seemed late on a train and you could talk like that.

He looked at me. "It's not clear," he said. "In the eyes of men or the eyes of God?" I must have been looking serious, because he added, "No. I'm not married. Nearly happened once, but no, it was the timing, and now I've got plenty to do."

"Oh," I said.

"It was a girl at Hilman," he said. "I'd have done it too, but it got away from us. There's a time for it and you can wait too long." He pointed at me. "You and Allison talking about it?"

"No, not really. I mean, I don't know. I guess we are, kind of, being over here together. But we've never talked about it really." Now he was just smiling at me, the kid. That's what I wanted to say: hey, I'm a kid here; I'm too young. I'm too young for anything.

Porter drank. He was the first person I'd met who drank heavily and didn't make a mess. When the guys in the dorm drank the way he did every night we saw him, you wouldn't see them for three days. "Well, just remember there's a time and if it gets away, it's gone. Be alert." It sounded so true what he said. I'd never had a talk like this on a train and it all sounded true. It had weight. I wondered if the time had come and gone. I thought about Allison at thirty or forty, teaching art history at Holyoke or someplace. She'd be married to someone else, a man who appeared to be older than she, some guy with a thin gray beard.

"How do you know if the time is right or if the time is coming up? How do you know about this timing?" I held out my beautiful white coffee cup, and Porter carefully filled it with the silver liquid. My future seemed vast, unchartable. "Whose fault was it when you lost this girl?"

Porter rolled his head to look at me. He looked serious. "Hers. Mine. She could have fixed it." He gave me a dire, ironic look. "And then it was too late."

"What was her name?"

"It's no longer important."

"Was she a Lake?"

The window with the cabin lights dimmed was a dreamy plate of our faint reflection torn up by all the white and yellow lights of industrial lots and truck parks. "Yeah," he said. "They all were. She wore her hair like Allison does and she looked that way." He had grown wistful and turned quickly to me with a grin. "Oh, hell, they all look that way when they're twenty-two." After a while, Porter sat up and again topped my cup with vodka.

In Edinburgh, we had to change trains. It was just before dawn, and I felt torn up by all the drinking. Porter walked me across to our connection, the train for Cape Wrath, and he went off—for some reason—to the stationmaster's office. Checking on something. He was going to make a few calls and then we'd be off again, north to the coast. I'd wanted to call Allison, but what would I say? I missed her? It was true, but it sounded like kid stuff somehow. It bothered me that there was nothing appropriate to say, nothing fitting, and the days themselves felt like they didn't fit, like I was waiting to grow into them. I sat sulking on the train in Edinburgh station. I was sure—that is, I suspected—that there was something wrong with me. I hadn't seen a fire or found a body or stopped a fight or *been* in one, really, nor could I say what was going to happen, because I could not read any of the signs. I wanted with all my teeth for something real to claim me. Anyway, that's as close as I can say it.

When Porter came back I could see him striding down the platform in the gray light like a man with a purpose. He didn't seem very drunk. He had a blue package under his arm. "Oh, matey, bad luck," he said, sitting opposite me in our new compartment. It was an older train, everything carpet and tassels and wood in remarkably good condition. It was like a time warp I was in, sitting there drunk while Porter told me he was going back to London. "Have to." He tapped the package. "They've overnighted all the data and I've got to compose the piece by tomorrow." He shook my hand heartily. "Wish me luck. And good luck to you. You'll love Cape Wrath. I once saw a submarine there off the coast. Good luck to you and your Gulf Stream." He smiled oddly with that last, a surreal look, I thought from my depth or height, distance anyway, and he was gone.

Well, I couldn't think. For a while I worked my face with my hands, carefully hoping that such a reasonable gesture might wake me, help me get a grip. But even after the train moved and then moved again, gaining momentum now, I was blank. Outside now the world was gray and green, the misting precipitation cutting the visibility to five hundred feet. This was part of a typical spring low pressure that would engulf all of Great Britain for a week. I didn't really know if I wanted to go on alone, but then I didn't know where I was going. I didn't know if I wanted to get off the train, because I didn't really know why I was on the train in the first place. I felt a little sick, a kind of shocky jangling that would resolve itself into nausea but not for about an hour, and so I put my feet on the opposite seat, closed my eyes, and waited.

Porter had been to our flat once. It was the day I had gone to the Royal Weather Offices in London, and when I came back, he and Allison were drinking our Whitbred at the tiny table. The place was a bed-sitter, too small for three people. I sat on the bed, but even so every time one of us moved the other two had to shift. Evidently Porter had come to invite us to some funky bar, the last mod pub off Piccadilly, he said. Allison's face was rosy in the close room. I told them about my day, the tour I'd taken, and Porter got me talking about El Niño, and I got a little carried away, I guess. I mean, I knew this stuff. But I remember them exchanging glances and smiling. I was smiling too, and I remember being happy waving my arms around as the great cycles of the English climate.

Now I felt every ripple of every steel track as it connected to the one before it, and I knew with increasing certainty that I was going to be sick. But there was something more than all the drink rising in me. Something was wrong. I was used to that feeling, that is, that things were not exactly as I expected, but this was something else. That blue package that Porter had carried back. I'd seen it all night, the corner of it, sticking out of the blown zipper of his leather valise. He'd had it all along. What was he talking about?

It was like that for forty minutes, my stomach roiling steadily, until we stopped at Pitlochry. When I stood up, I felt the whole chemistry seize, and I limped to the loo and after a band of sweat burst onto my forehead, I was sick, voluminously sick, and then I was better, that is, just stricken not poisoned. My head felt empty. I hurried to the platform and wrangled with the telephone until I was able to reach Roger Ardreprice. I had tried Allison at home and at the museum, and then I called Roger at work and a woman answered the phone: "Keats's House."

"Listen," I started after he'd come to the phone. Then I didn't know what to say. Why was I calling? "Listen," I said again. "I'm uneasy about something. . . ."

"Where are you calling from?" he asked.

"I'm in Scotland. I'm in someplace, Pitlochry. Porter and I were going north to the coast."

"Porter, oh, for god's sakes, you didn't get tangled up with Porter, did you? What's he got you doing? I should have said something."

The phone box was close, airless, and I pressed the red-paned door open with my foot. "He's been great, but . . ."

"Oh my, this is bad news. Porter, for your information, probably started the Lake fire. He was tried for it, you know. He is bloody bad news. You keep yourself and that young woman away from him. Especially the girl. What's her name?"

I set my forehead against one of the glass panes of the phone booth and breathed through my mouth deeply two or three times. "Allison," I said.

"Right," Roger Ardreprice said from London. "Don't let him at her."

I couldn't hear very well now, a kind of static had set up in my head, and I set the phone back on the cradle.

The return train was a lesson in sanity. I felt the whole time that I would go crazy the next minute, and this powerful about-to-explode feeling finally became a granite rock which I held on my lap with my traveling case. I thought if I could sit still, everything would be all right. As the afternoon failed, I sat perfectly still through the maddening countryside, across the bridges and rivers of Great Britain with my body feeling distant and infirm in the waxy shadow of my hangover. Big decisions, I learned that day, are made in the body, and my body recoiled at the thought of Porter.

From King's Cross I took a cab to the museum. I didn't care about the expense. It was odd then, being in a hurry for the first time that spring, impatient with the old city, which now seemed just a place in my way. Allison wasn't there. I called home. No answer. I checked in the Museum Pub, where we'd had lunch a dozen times; those lunches all seemed a long time ago. I grabbed another taxi and went home. Our narrow flat seemed like a bittersweet joke: what children lived here? The light rain had followed me south, as I knew it would, and in the mist I walked up to the High Street and had a doner kebab. It tasted good and I ate it as I drifted down to the tube stop. There was no hurry now. Rumbling through the Underground in the yellow light, I let my shoulders roll with the train. Everyone looked tired, hungover, ready for therapy.

I'd never been to the Hotel Eden alone, and in the new dark in the quiet rain, I stood a moment and took it in. It was frankly just a sad old four-story white building, the two columns on each side of the doors peeling as they had for years on end. Norris was inside alone, and I took a pint of lager from him and sat at one of the little tables. The beer nailed me back in place. I was worn out and spent, but I was through being sick. I had another pint as I watched Norris move in the back bar. It would be three hours before Allison and Porter came in from wherever they were, and then I would tell them all about my trip to Scotland. It would be my first story.

KEITH

THEY WERE LAB partners. It was that simple, how they met. She was *the* Barbara Anderson, president of half the school offices and queen of the rest. He was Keith Zetterstrom, a character, an oddball, a Z. His name was called last. The spring of their senior year at their equipment drawer she spoke to him for the first time in all their grades together: "Are you my lab partner?"

He spread the gear on the counter for the inventory and looked at her. "Yes, I am," he said. "I haven't lied to you this far, and I'm not going to start now."

After school Barbara Anderson met her boyfriend, Brian Woodworth, in the parking lot. They had twin red scooters because Brian had given her one at Christmas. "That guy," Barbara said, pointing to where Keith stood in the bus line, "is my lab partner."

"Who is he?" Brian said.

Keith was the window, wallpaper, woodwork. He'd been

there for years and they'd never seen him. This was complicated because for years he was short and then he grew tall. And then he grew a long black slash of hair and now he had a crewcut. He was hard to see, hard to fix in one's vision.

The experiments in chemistry that spring concerned states of matter, and Barbara and Keith worked well together, quietly and methodically testing the elements.

"You're Barbara Anderson," he said finally as they waited for a beaker to boil. "We were on the same kickball team in fourth grade and I stood behind you in the sixth-grade Christmas play. I was a Russian soldier."

Barbara Anderson did not know what to say to these things. She couldn't remember the sixth-grade play . . . and fourth grade? So she said, "What are you doing after graduation?"

"The sky's the limit," he said. "And you are going off to Brown University."

"How did you know that?"

"The list has been posted for weeks."

"Oh. Right. Well, I may go to Brown and I may stay here and go to the university with my boyfriend."

Their mixture boiled and Keith poured some off into a cooling tray. "So what do you do?" he asked her.

Barbara eyed him. She was used to classmates having curiosity about her, and she had developed a pleasant condescension, but Keith had her off guard.

"What do you mean?"

"On a date with Brian, your boyfriend. What do you do?"

"Lots of things. We play miniature golf."

"You go on your scooters and play miniature golf."

"Yes."

"Is there a windmill?"

"Yes, there's a windmill. Why do you ask? What are you getting at?"

"Who wins? The golf."

"Brian," Barbara said. "He does."

BARBARA SHOWED THE note to Trish, her best friend.

REASONS YOU SHOULD GO WITH ME

A.   You are my lab partner.

B.   Just to see. (You too, even Barbara Anderson, contain the same restless germ of curiosity that all humanity possesses, a trait that has led us out of the complacency of our dark caves into the bright world where we invented bowling—among other things.)

C.   It's not a "date."

"Great," Trish said. "We certainly believe this! But, girl, who wants to graduate without a night out with a bald whatever. And I don't think he's going to ravish you—against your will, that is. Go for it. We'll tell Brian that you're staying at my house."

KEITH DROVE A Chevy pickup, forest-green, and when Barbara climbed in, she asked, "Why don't you drive this to school?"

"There's a bus. I love the bus. Have you ever been on one?"

"Not a school bus."

"Oh, try it," he said. "Try it. It's so big and it doesn't drop you off right at your house."

"You're weird."

"Why? Oh, does the bus go right to your house? Come on, does it? But you've got to admit they're big, and that yellow paint job? Show me that somewhere else, I dare you. Fasten your seat belt, let's go."

The evening went like this: Keith turned onto Bloomfield, the broad business avenue that stretched from near the airport all the way back to the university, and he told her, "I want you to point out your least favorite building on this street."

"So we're not going bowling?"

"No, we're saving that. I thought we'd just get a little something to eat. So, keep your eyes open. Any places you can't stand?" By the time they reached the airport, Barbara had pointed out four she thought were ugly. When they turned around, Keith added: "Now, your final choice, please. And not someplace you just don't like. We're looking for genuine aversion."

Barbara selected a five-story metal building near downtown, with a simple marquee above the main doors that read INSUR-ANCE.

"Excellent," Keith said as he swung the pickup to the curb. He began unloading his truck. "This is truly garish. The architect here is now serving time."

"This is where my father used to work."

Keith paused, his arms full of equipment. "When . . ."

"When he divorced my mom. His office was right up there." She pointed. "I hate driving by this place."

"Good," Keith said with renewed conviction. "Come over here and sit down. Have a Coke."

Barbara sat in a chaise longue that Keith had set on the flood-lit front lawn next to a folding table. He handed her a Coke. "We're eating here?"

"Yes, miss," he said, toting over the cooler and the little propane stove. "It's rustic but traditional: cheese omelets and hash brown potatoes. Sliced tomatoes for a salad with choice of dressing, and—for dessert—ice cream. On the way home, of course." Keith poured some oil into the frying pan. "There is nothing like a meal to alter the chemistry of a place."

On the way home, they did indeed stop for ice cream, and Barbara asked him: "Wasn't your hair long last year, like in your face and down like this?" She swept her hand past his eye.

"It was."

"Why is it so short now?"

Keith ran his hand back over his head. "Seasonal cut. Summer's a-coming in. I want to lead the way."

It was an odd week for Barbara. She actually did feel different about the insurance building as she drove her scooter by it on the way to school. When Trish found out about dinner, she said, "That was you! I saw your spread as we headed down to Barney's. You were like camped out, right?"

Wonder spread on Barbara's face as she thought it over. "Yeah, it was cool. He cooked."

"Right. But please, I've known a lot of guys who cook and they were some of the slickest. *High School Confidential* says: 'There are three million seductions and only one goal.'"

"You're a cynic."

"Cynicism is a useful survival skill."

In chemistry, it was sulfur. Liquid, solid, and gas. The hallways of the chemistry annex smelled like rotten eggs and jokes abounded. Barbara winced through the white wispy smoke as Keith stirred the melting sulfur nuggets.

"This is awful," Barbara said.

"This is wonderful," Keith said. "This is the exact smell that greets sinners at the gates of hell. They think it's awful; here we get to enjoy it for free."

Barbara looked at him. "My lab partner is a certifiable . . ."

"Your lab partner will meet you tonight at seven o'clock."

"Keith," she said, taking the stir stick from him and prodding the undissolved sulfur, "I'm dating Brian. Remember?"

"Good for you," he said. "Now tell me something I don't know. Listen: I'll pick you up at seven. This isn't a date. This isn't dinner. This is errands. I'm serious. Necessary errands—for your friends."

Barbara Anderson rolled her eyes.

"You'll be home by nine. Young Mr. Brian can scoot by then. I mean it." Keith leaned toward her, the streams of baking acrid sulfur rising past his face. "I'm not lying to you."

WHEN SHE GOT to the truck that night, Keith asked her, "What did you tell Brian?"

"I told him I had errands at my aunt's and to come by at ten for a little while."

"That's awfully late on a school night."

"Keith."

"I mean, why didn't you tell him you'd be with me for two hours?" He looked at her. "I have trouble lending credibility to a relationship that is almost one year old and one in which one of the members has given another an actual full-size, roadworthy motor vehicle, and yet it remains a relationship in which one of the members lies to the other when she plans to spend two hours with her lab partner, a person with whom she has inhaled the very vapors of hell."

"Stop the truck, Keith. I'm getting out."

"And miss bowling? And miss the search for bowling balls?"

Half an hour later they were in Veteran's Thrift, reading the bowling balls. They'd already bought five at Desert Industry Thrift Shops and the Salvation Army store. Keith's rule was it had to be less than two dollars. They already had PATTY for Trish, BETSY and KIM for two more of Barbara's friends, an initialled ball B.R. for Brian even though his last name was Woodworth ("Puzzle him," Keith said. "Make him guess"), and WALT for their chemistry teacher, Mr. Walter Miles. They found three more in the bins in Veteran's Thrift, one marked SKIP, one marked COSMO ("A must," Keith said), and a brilliant green ball, run deeply with hypnotic swirls, which had no name at all.

Barbara was touring the wide shelves of used appliances, toys, and kitchen utensils. "Where do they get all this stuff?"

"You've never been in a secondhand store before, have you?"

"No. Look at all this stuff. This is a quarter?" She held up a large plastic tray with the Beatles' pictures on it.

"That," Keith said, taking it from her and placing it in the cart with their bowling balls, "came from the home of a fan of the first magnitude. Oh, it's a sad story. It's enough to say that this is here tonight because of Yoko Ono." Keith's attention was taken by a large trophy, standing among the dozen other trophies on the top shelf. "Whoa," he said, pulling it down. It was huge, over three feet tall: six golden columns, ascending from a white marble base to a silver obelisk, framed by two embossed silver wreaths, and topped by a silver woman on a rearing motorcycle. The inscription on the base read: WIDOWMAKER HILL CLIMB — FIRST PLACE 1987. Keith held it out to show Barbara, like a man holding a huge bottle of aspirin in a television commercial. "But this is another story altogether." He placed it reverently in the basket.

"And that would be?"

"No time. You've got to get back and meet Brian, a person who doesn't know where you are." Keith led her to the checkout. He was quiet all the way to the truck. He placed the balls carefully in the cardboard boxes in the truck bed and then set the huge trophy between them on the seat.

"You don't know where this trophy came from."

Keith put a finger to his lips—*"Shhhh"*—and started the truck and headed to Barbara's house. After several blocks of silence, Barbara folded her arms. "It's a tragic, tragic story," he said in a low voice. "I mean, this girl was a golden girl, an angel, the light in everybody's life."

"Do I want to hear this tragic story?"

"She was a wonder. Straight A's, with an A plus in chemistry. The girl could do no wrong. And then," Keith looked at Barbara, "she got involved with motorcycles."

"Is this her on top of the trophy?"

"The very girl." Keith nodded grimly. "Oh, it started innocently enough with a little red motor scooter, a toy really, and she could be seen running errands for the Ladies' Society and other charities every Saturday and Sunday when she wasn't home studying." Keith turned to Barbara, moving the trophy forward so he could see her. "I should add here that her fine academic standing got her into Brown University, where she was going that fateful fall." Keith laid the trophy back. "When her thirst for speed grew and grew, breaking over her good common sense like a tidal wave, sending her into the arms of a twelve-hundred-cc Harley-Davidson, one of the most powerful two-wheeled vehicles in the history of mankind." They turned onto Barbara's street, and suddenly Barbara ducked, her head against Keith's knee.

"Drive by," she whispered. "Just keep going."

"What?" Keith said. "If I do that Brian won't see you." Keith could see Brian leaning against his scooter in the driveway. "Is that guy always early?"

Keith turned the next corner, and Barbara sat up and opened her door. "I'll go down the alley."

"Cool," Keith said. "So you sneak down the alley to meet your boyfriend? Pretty sexy."

She gave him a look.

"Okay, have fun. But there's one last thing, partner. I'll pick you up at four to deliver these bowling balls."

"Four?"

"Four a.m. Brian will be gone, won't he?"

"Keith."

"It's not a date. We've got to finish this program, right?"

Barbara looked over at Brian and quickly back at Keith as she opened the truck door. "Okay, but meet me at the corner. There," she pointed, "by the postbox."

SHE WAS THERE. The streets of the suburbs were dark and quiet, everything in its place, sleeping, but Barbara Anderson stood in the humming lamplight, humming her elbows. It was eerily quiet and she could hear Keith coming for two or three blocks before he turned onto her street. He had the heater on in the truck, and when she climbed in he handed her a blue cardigan, which she quickly buttoned up. "Four a.m.," she said, rubbing her hands over the air vent. "Now this is weird out here."

"Yeah," Keith said. "Four o'clock makes it a different planet. I recommend it. But bring a sweater." He looked at her. "You look real sleepy," he said. "You look good. This is the face you ought to bring to school."

Barbara looked at Keith and smiled. "No makeup, okay? It's

four a.m." His face looked tired, and in the pale dash lights, with his short, short hair he looked more like a child, a little boy. "What do we do?"

"We give each of these babies," Keith nodded back at the bowling balls in the truck bed, "a new home."

They delivered the balls, placing them carefully on the porches of their friends, including Trish and Brian, and then they spent half an hour finding Mr. Miles's house, which was across town, a tan split-level. Keith handed Barbara the ball marked WALT and made her walk it up to the front porch. When she returned to the truck, Keith said, "Years from now you'll be able to say, 'When I was seventeen I put a bowling ball on my chemistry's teacher's front porch.'"

"His name was Walt," Barbara added.

At five-thirty, as the first gray light rose, Barbara Anderson and Keith walked into Jewel's Café carrying the last two balls: the green beauty and COSMO. Jewel's was the oldest café in the city, an all-night diner full of mailmen. "So," Barbara said, as they slid into one of the huge maroon booths, "who gets these last two?" She was radiant now, fully awake, and energized by the new day.

The waitress appeared and they ordered Round-the-World omelettes, hash browns, juice, milk, coffee, and wheat muffins, and Barbara ate with gusto, looking up halfway through. "So, where next?" She saw his plate. "Hey, you're not eating."

Keith looked odd, his face milky, his eyes gray. "This food is full of the exact amino acids to have a certifiably chemical day," he said. "I'll get around to it."

But he never did. He pushed his plate to the side and turned the place mat over and began to write on it.

"Are you feeling all right?" Barbara said.

"I'm okay."

She tilted her head at him skeptically.

"Hey. I'm okay. I haven't lied to you this far. Why would I start now? You know I'm okay, don't you? Well? Don't you think I'm okay?"

She looked at him and said quietly: "You're okay."

He showed her the note he had written:

Dear Waitress: My girlfriend and I are from rival families— different sides of the tracks, races, creeds, colors, and zip codes, and if they found out we had been out bowling all night, they would banish us to prison schools on separate planets. Please, please find a good home for our only bowling balls. Our enormous sadness is only mitigated by the fact that we know you'll take care of them.

With sweet sorrow—COSMO

In the truck, Barbara said, "Mitigated?"

"Always leave them something to look up."

"You're sick, aren't you?" she said.

"You look good in that sweater," he said. When she started to remove it, he added, "Don't. I'll get it after class, in just," he looked at his watch, "two hours and twenty minutes."

BUT HE WASN'T there. He wasn't there all week. The class did experiments with oxidation and Mr. Miles spent two days explaining and diagramming rust. On Friday, Mr. Miles worked with Barbara on the experiments and she asked him what was wrong with Keith. "I'm not sure," her teacher told her. "But I think he's on medication."

Barbara had a tennis match on Tuesday afternoon at school, and Brian picked her up and drove her home. Usually he came in for an hour or so on these school days and they made out a little and raided the fridge, but for the first time she begged off, claiming homework, kissing him on the cheek and running into her house. But on Friday, during her away match at Viewmont, she felt odd again. She knew Brian was in the stands. When she walked off the court after the match it was nearly dark and Brian was waiting. She gave Trish her rackets and Barbara climbed on Brian's scooter without a word. "You weren't that bad," he said. "Viewmont always has a good team."

"Brian, let's just go home."

"You want to stop at Swenson's, get something to eat?"

"No."

So Brian started his scooter and drove them home. Barbara could tell by the way he was driving that he was mad, and it confused her: she felt strangely glad about it. She didn't want to invite him in, let him grope her on the couch. She held on as he took the corners too fast and slipped through the stop signs, but all the way home she didn't put her chin on his shoulder.

At her house, she got the scene she'd been expecting. "Just what is the matter with you?" Brian said. For some reason when he'd gone to kiss her, she'd averted her face. Her heart burned with pleasure and shame. She was going to make up a lie about tennis, but then just said, "Oh Brian. Just leave me alone for a while, will you? Just go home."

Inside, she couldn't settle down. She didn't shower or change clothes. She sat in the dark of her room for a while and then, using only the tiny spot of her desk lamp, she copied her chemistry notes for the week and called Trish.

It was midnight when Trish picked her up quietly by the mailbox on the corner. Trish was smoking one of her Marlboros and blowing smoke into the windshield. She said, *"High School Confidential,* Part Five: Young Barbara Anderson, still in her foxy tennis clothes, and her old friend Trish meet again at midnight, cruise the Strip, pick up two young men with tattoos, and are never seen alive again. Is that it? Count me in."

"Not quite. It goes like this: two sultry babes, one of whom has just been a royal bitch to her boyfriend for no reason, drive to 1147 Fairmont to drop off the week's chemistry notes."

"That would be Keith Zetterstrom's address, I'd guess." Trish said.

"He's my lab partner."

"Of course he is," Trish said.

"He missed all last week. Mr. Miles told me that Keith's on medication."

"Oh my god!" Trish clamped the steering wheel. "He's got cancer. That's that scary hairdo. He's sick."

"No he doesn't. I checked the college lists. He's going to Dickinson."

"Not for long, honey. I should have known this." Trish inhaled and blew smoke thoughtfully out of the side of her mouth. "Bald kids in high school without earrings have got cancer."

KEITH WAS IN class the following Monday for the chemistry exam: sulfur and rust. After class, Barbara Anderson took him by the arm and led him to her locker. "Thanks for the notes, partner," he said. "They were absolutely chemical. I aced the quiz."

"You were sick last week."

"Last week." He pondered. "Oh, you mean because I wasn't

here. What do you do, come every day? I just couldn't; it would take away the something special I feel for this place. I like to come from time to time and keep the dew on the rose, so to speak."

"I know what's the matter with you."

"Good for you, Barbara Anderson. And I know what's the matter with you too; sounds like a promising relationship."

Barbara pulled his folded sweater from the locker and handed it to him. As she did, Brian came up and said to them both: "Oh, I see." He started to walk away.

"Brian," Keith said. "Listen. You don't see. I'm not a threat to you. How could I be a threat to you? Think about it." Brian stood, his eyes narrowed. Keith went on: "Barbara's not stupid. What am I going to do, trick her? I'm her lab partner in chemistry. Relax." Keith went to Brian and took his hand, shook it. "I'm serious, Woodworth."

Brian stood for a moment longer until Barbara said, "I'll see you at lunch," and then he backed and disappeared down the hall. When he was gone, Barbara said, "*Are* you tricking me?"

"I don't know. Something's going on. I'm a little confused."

"You're confused. Who are you? Where have you been, Keith Zetterstrom? I've been going to school with you all these years and I've never even seen you and then we're delivering bowling balls together and now you're sick. Where were you last year? What are you doing? What are you going to do next year?"

"Last year I got a C in Spanish with Mrs. Whitehead. It was gruesome. This year is somewhat worse, with a few exceptions, and all in all, I'd say the sky is the limit." Keith took her wrist. "Quote me on that."

Barbara took a sharp breath through her nose and quietly began to cry.

"Oh, let's not," Keith said, pushing a handkerchief into her hand. "Here. Think of this." He moved her back against the wall, out of the way of students passing by. "If I was having a good year, I might never have spoken to you. Extreme times require extreme solutions. I went all those years sitting in the back and then I had to get sick to start talking. Now that's something, isn't it? Besides, I've got a plan. I'll pick you up at nine. Listen: bring your pajamas and a robe."

Barbara looked at him over the handkerchief."

"Hey. Trust me. You were the one who was crying. I'll see you at nine o'clock. This will cheer you up."

THE HOSPITAL WAS on the hill, and Keith parked in the farthest corner of the vast parking lot, one hundred yards from the nearest car. Beneath them in the dark night, the city teemed and shimmered, a million lights.

"It looks like a city on another planet," Barbara Anderson said as she stepped out of the truck.

"It does, indeed," Keith said, grabbing his bag. "Now if we only knew if the residents are friendly." He took her arm. "And now I'm going to cheer you up. I'm going to take you in that building," Keith pointed at the huge hospital, lit like an ocean liner in the night, "and buy you a package of gum."

They changed clothes in the fifth-floor restrooms and met in the hallway, in pajamas and robes, and stuffed their street clothes into Barbara's tennis bag.

"Oh, I feel better already," Barbara said.

"Now take my arm like this," Keith moved next to her and placed her hand above his elbow, "and look down like this." He put his chin on his chest. Barbara tried it. "No, not such a sad

face, more serious, be strong. Good. Now walk just like this, little stab steps, real slow."

They started down the hallway, creeping along one side.
"How far is it?" Barbara said. People passed them walking quietly in groups of two or three. It was the end of visiting hours.
"A hundred yards to the elevators and down three floors, then
out a hundred more. Keep your face down."

"Are people looking at us?"

"Well, yes. They've never seen a braver couple. And they've
never seen such chemical pajamas. What are those little deals,
lambs?"

They continued along the windows, through the lobby and
down the elevator, in which they stood side by side, their four
hands clasped together, while they were looking at their tennis
shoes. The other people in the car gave them room out of respect. The main hall was worse, thick with people, everyone
going five miles an hour faster than Barbara and Keith, who
shuffled along whispering.

In the gift shop, finally, they parted the waters. The small
room was crowded, but the people stepped aside and Keith and
Barbara stood right at the counter. "A package of chewing gum,
please," Keith said.

"Which kind?" said the candy striper.

"Sugarless. My sister and I want our teeth to last forever."

THEY RAN TO the truck, leaping and swinging their arms.
Keith threw the bag containing their clothes into the truck bed
and climbed into the cab. Barbara climbed in, laughing, and
Keith said, "Come on, face the facts: you feel better! You're
cured!" And she slid across the seat meaning to hug him but it

changed for both of them and they kissed. She pulled him to her side and they kissed again, one of her arms around his neck and one of her hands on his face. They fell into a spin there in the truck, eyes closed, holding on to each other in their pajamas, her robe open, their heads against the backseat, kissing. Barbara shifted and Keith sat up; the look they exchanged held. Below them the city's lights flickered. Barbara cupped her hand carefully on the top of Keith's bald scalp. She pulled him forward and they kissed. When she looked in his eyes again she knew what was going to happen, and it was a powerful feeling that gave her strange new certainty as she went for his mouth again.

There were other moments that surfaced in the truck in the night above the ancient city. Something Keith did, his hand reminded her of Brian, and then that thought vanished as they were beyond Brian in a moment. Later, well beyond even her notions of what to do and what not to do, lathered and breathing as if in toil, she heard herself say, "Yes." She said that several times.

SHE LOOKED FOR Keith everywhere, catching glimpses of his head, his shoulder, in the hallways. In chemistry they didn't talk; there were final reports, no need to work together. Finally, three days before graduation, they stood side by side cleaning out their chemistry equipment locker, waiting for Mr. Miles to check them off. Keith's manner was what? Easy, too confident, too neutral. He seemed to take up too much space in the room. She hated the way he kept his face blank and open, as if fishing for the first remark. She held off, feeling the restraint as a physical pang. Mr. Miles inventoried their cupboard and asked for their keys. He had a large ring of thirty or forty of the thin brass keys. Keith handed his to Mr. Miles and then Barbara Anderson found her key in the side of her purse and handed it to the teacher. She hated relinquishing the key; it was the only thing she had that meant she would see Keith, and now with it gone something opened in her and it hurt in a way she'd never hurt before. Keith turned to her and seeing something in her face, shrugged and said, "The end of chemistry as we know it. Which isn't really very well."

"Who are you?" Barbara said, her voice a kind of surprise to her. "You're so glib. Such a little actor." Mr. Miles looked up from his check sheet and several students turned toward them. Barbara was speaking loudly; she couldn't help it. "What are you doing to me? If you ask me this is a pretty chickenshit good-bye." Everyone was looking at her. Then her face would not work at all, the tears coming from some hot place, and Barbara Anderson walked from the room.

Keith hadn't moved. Mr. Miles looked at Keith, alarmed. Keith whispered: "Don't worry, Mr. Miles. She was addressing her remarks to me."

THERE WAS ONE more scene. The night before graduation, while her classmates met in the bright, noisy gym for the year-book-signing party, Barbara drove out to the airport and met Keith where he said he'd be: at the last gate, H-17. There on an empty stretch of maroon carpet in front of three large banks of seats full of travelers, he was waiting. He handed her a pretty green canvas valise and an empty paper ticket sleeve.

"You can't even talk as yourself," she said. "You always need a setting. Now we're pretending I'm going somewhere?"

He looked serious tonight, weary. There were gray shadows under his eyes. "You wanted a goodbye scene," he said. "I tried not to do this."

"It's all a joke," she said. "You joke all the time."

"You know what my counselor said?" He smiled thinly as if glad to give her this point. "He said that this is a phase, that I'll stop joking soon." Their eyes met and the look held again. "Come here," he said. She stepped close to him. He put his hand on her elbow. "You want a farewell speech. Okay, here you go. You better call Brian and get your scooter back. Tell him I tricked you. Wake up, lady. Get real. I just wanted to see if I could give Barbara Anderson a whirl. And I did. It was selfish, okay? I just screwed you around a little. You said it yourself: it was a joke. That's my speech. How was it?"

"You didn't screw me around, Keith. You didn't give me a whirl." Barbara moved his hand and then put her arms around his neck so she could speak in his ear. She could see some of the people watching them. "You made love to me, Keith. It wasn't a joke. You made love to me and I met you tonight to say—good for you. Extreme times require extreme solutions." She was whispering as they stood alone on that carpet in their embrace. "I wondered how it was going to happen, but you were a surprise. Way to go. What did you think? That I wanted to go off to college an eighteen-year-old virgin? That pajama bit was great; I'll remember it." Now people were deplaning, entering the gate area and streaming around the young couple. Barbara felt Keith begin to tremble, and she closed her eyes. "It wasn't a joke. There's this: I made love to you too. You were there, re-member? I'm glad for it." She pulled back slightly and found his lips. For a moment she was keenly aware of the public scene they were making, but that disappeared and they twisted tighter and were just there, kissing. She had dropped the valise and when the mock ticket slipped from her fingers behind his neck, a young woman in a business suit knelt and retrieved it and tapped Barbara on the hand. Barbara clutched the ticket and dropped her head to Keith's chest.

"I remember," he said. "My memory is aces."

"Tell me, Keith," she said. "What are these people thinking? Make something up."

"No need. They've got it right. That's why we came out here. They think we're saying goodbye."

SIMPLY PUT, THAT was the last time Barbara Anderson saw Keith Zetterstrom. That fall when she arrived in Providence for her freshman year at Brown, there was one package waiting for her, a large trophy topped by a girl on a motorcycle. She had seen it before. She kept it in her dorm window, where it was visible four stories from the ground, and she told her roommates that it meant a lot to her, that it represented a lot of fun and hard work but her goal had been to win the Widowmaker Hill Climb, and once she had done that, she sold her bikes and gave up her motorcycles forever.

THE PRISONER OF
BLUESTONE

THERE WAS A camera. Mr. Ruckelbar was helping load the crushed sedan onto DiPaulo's tow truck when an old Nikon camera fell from the gashed trunkwell and hit him on the shoulder. At first he thought it was a rock or a taillight assembly; things had fallen on him before as he and DiPaulo had wrestled the ruined vehicles onto the tiltbed of DiPaulo's big custom Ford, and of course DiPaulo wasn't there to be hit. He had a bad back and was in the cab working the hydraulics and calling, "Good? Are we good yet?"

"Whoa, that's enough!" he called. Now Ruckelbar would have to clamber up and set the chains. DiPaulo, he thought, the wrecker with the bad back.

It was a thick gray twilight in the last week of October, chilly now with the sun gone. This vehicle had been out back for too long. The end of summer was always bad. After the Labor Day weekend, he always took in a couple cars. He stored them out in a fenced lot behind his Sunoco station, getting twenty dollars a week until the insurance paperwork was completed, all of them the same really, totaled and sold to DiPaulo, who took them out to Junk World, his four acres of damaged vehicles near Torrington. Ruckelbar was glad to see this silver Saab go. It had been weird having the kid almost every afternoon since it had arrived, sitting out in the crushed thing full of leaves and beads of glass, just sitting there until dark sometimes, then walking back toward town along the two-lane without a proper jacket, some boy, the brother he said he was, some kid you didn't need sitting in a totaled Saab, some skinny kid maybe fourteen years old.

Ruckelbar cinched the final chain hitch and climbed down. "What'd you get?" It was DiPaulo. The small old man had limped back in the new dark and had picked the camera up. "This has got to be worth something."

"It's that kid's. It was his sister's car."

DiPaulo handed him back the camera. "That kid. That kid doesn't need to see this. I'd chuck it in the river before I let him see it. He's nutty enough." DiPaulo shook his head. "What's he going to do when he sees the car is finally gone?"

"Lord knows," Ruckelbar said. "Maybe he'll find someplace else to go."

"Well, that car's been here a long time, summer's over, and that camera," DiPaulo poked it with one of his short stained fingers, "is long gone to everybody. Let you leave the sleeping dogs asleep. Just put it in a drawer. You listen to your old pal. Your father would." DiPaulo took Ruckelbar's shoulder in his hand for a second. "See you. I'll be back Wednesday for that van. You take care." The little old man turned one more time and pointed at Ruckelbar. "And for god's sakes, don't tell that kid where this car is going."

DiPaulo had known Ruckelbar's father, "for a thousand years

before you came along," he'd say, and Ruckelbar could remember DiPaulo saying "Leave sleeping dogs asleep" throughout the years in friendly arguments every time there was some sort of cash windfall. The elder Ruckelbar would smile and say that DiPaulo should have been a tax attorney.

After DiPaulo left, Ruckelbar rolled the wooden desk chair back inside the office of the Sunoco station and locked up. The building was a local landmark really, such an old little stone edifice painted blue, sitting all alone out on Route 21, where the woods had grown up around it and made it appear a hut in a fairy tale, with two gas pumps. The Bluestone everyone called it, and it was used to mark the quarry turnoff; "four miles past the Bluestone." It certainly marked Ruckelbar's life, was his life. He had met Clare at a community bonfire at the Quarry Meadows when she was still a student at Woodbine Prep, and above there at the Upper Quarry, remote and private, one night a year later she had helped him undo both of them in his father's truck and urgently had begun a sex life that wouldn't last five years.

Ruckelbar was a sophomore at the University of Massachusetts when his father had a heart attack in the station that March and died sitting up against the wall in the single-bay garage. Ruckelbar was twenty and when he came home it would stick. Clare was back from Sarah Lawrence that summer, and it was all right for a while, even good, the way anything can be good when you're young. It was fun having a service station, and after closing they'd go to the pubs beyond the blue-collar town of Garse, roadhouses that are all gone now. It was thrilling for Clare to sit in his pickup, the station truck, the same truck in which she arched herself against him at Upper Quarry and the same truck he drives now, as he rocked the huge set of keys in

the latch of Bluestone and then extracted them and turned to her
for a night. But she didn't think he was serious about it. He was
to be an engineer; his father had said as much, and then another
year passed, his mother now ill, while he ran the place all winter,
plowing the snow from around the station with a blade on the
old truck that his father had welded himself. When spring came
it was a done deal. The wild iris and the dogwoods burst from
every seam in the earth and the world changed for Ruckelbar,
his sense of autonomy and worth, and he knew he was here for
life. Even by the time they married, Clare had had enough.
When she saw that the little baby girl she had the next year gave
her no leverage with him, she stopped coming out with box
lunches and avoided driving by the place even when she had to
drive to Garse going by way of Tipton, which added four miles
to the trip. She let him know that she didn't want to hear about
Bluestone in her house and that he was to leave his overalls at
the station, his boots in the garage, and he was to shower in the
basement.

He'd gone along with this somehow, gone along without an
angry word, without many words at all, the separate bedroom in
the nice house in Corbett, and now after nearly twenty years,
it was their way. After the loss of Clare and then the loss of
the memory of her in his truck and in his bed came the loss of
his daughter, which he also just allowed. Clare had her at home
and Clare was determined that Marjorie should understand the
essential elements of disappointment, and the lessons started
with his name. Now, at seventeen, Marjorie was a day student at
Woodbine, the prep school in Corbett, and her name was Marjorie Bar, shortened Clare said for convenience and for her
career, whatever it would be. And Ruckelbar had let that hap-

pen too. He could fix any feature of any automobile, truck, or element of farm equipment, but he could not fix this.

AT HOME AFTER a silent dinner with Clare, he broke the rule about talking about the station and told her that DiPaulo had picked up the car, the one the boy had been sitting in every day for weeks. She didn't like DiPaulo—he'd always been part of the way her life had betrayed her—and she let her eyes lift in disgust and then asked about the boy, "What did he do?" They were clearing the supper dishes. Marjorie ate dinner at school and arrived home after the evening study hall. It was queer that Clare should ask a question, and Ruckelbar, who hadn't intended his comment to begin a conversation, was surprised and not sure of how he should answer.

"He sat in the car. In the driver's seat."

This stopped Clare midstep and she held her dishes still. "All day?"

"He came after school and walked home after dark." It was the most Ruckelbar had spoken about the station in his kitchen for five or six years. Clare resumed sorting out the silverware and wiping up. Ruckelbar realized he wanted to ask Clare what to do about the camera. "Do you remember the accident?" he asked. "The girl?"

"If it's the same girl. The three young people from Garse. She was a tramp. They were killed on Labor Day or just before. They went off the quarry road."

Ruckelbar, who hadn't seen the papers, had known about the accident, of course. The police tow truck driver had told him about the three students, and the vehicle was crushed in so radical a fashion anyone could see it had fallen some distance onto the rock. Clare seemed to know more about it, something she'd read or heard, but Ruckelbar didn't know how to ask, and in a moment the chance was lost.

"Who's a tramp?" Marjorie entered the kitchen, putting her bookbag on a chair.

"Your father has some lowlife living in a car."

Ruckelbar looked at her.

"Any pie?" Marjorie asked her mother. Clare extracted a pumpkin pie from the fridge. Under the plastic wrap, it was uncut, one of Clare's fresh pumpkin pies. Ruckelbar looked at it, just a pie, and he stopped slipping. He'd already exited the room in his head, and he came back. "I'd like a piece of that pie, too, Clare. If I could please."

"You didn't get any?" Marjorie said. "You must really smell like gasoline tonight." She was actually trying to be light.

"He's not a lowlife, Clare," he said to her as she set a wedge of pie before him and dropped a fork onto the table. Even Marjorie, who had silently sided with her mother every time she'd had the chance, looked up in surprise at Clare. "It's the boy whose sister was killed last summer."

"Sheila Morton," Marjorie said.

"The tramp," Clare said.

Ruckelbar took a bite of pie. He was going to stay right here. This was the scene he'd drifted away from a thousand times. They were talking.

"She was not a tramp," he said. "This boy is a nice boy."

"He's disturbed," Clare said. "God, going out there to sit in the car?"

"Sheila was a slut," Marjorie said. "Everybody knew that."

The moment had gone very strange for all of them together like this in the kitchen. An ordinary night would have found Ruckelbar in the garage or his bedroom, Marjorie on the phone, and Clare at the television. They all felt the vague uncertainty of having the rules shift. No one would leave and no one knew how it would end; this was all new.

"She was, Dad," Marjorie said, setting Ruckelbar back in his chair with the word "Dad," which in its disuse had become monumental, naked and direct. They all heard it. Marjorie went on, "She put out, okay? One of those guys was from Woodbine. What do you think they were doing? They were headed for the Upper Quarry. It's where the sluts go. You don't try that road unless you're going to put out."

Ruckelbar had stopped eating the pie. He put down his fork and turned: Clare was gone.

A SUNNY SATURDAY in New England the last day in October: Ruckelbar lives for days like these, maybe this day in particular, the sun even at noon fallen away hard, but the lever of heat still there, though more than half the leaves are down and they skirl across Route 21 and pool against the banks of old grass. Ruckelbar sits in his old wooden office chair, which he pulls out front on days just like this, the whole scene a throwback to any fall afternoon thirty years ago, that being Clare's word, "throwback," but for now he's free in what feels like the very last late sunlight of the year. It's Halloween, he remembers; tonight they turn their clocks back. It doesn't matter. For now, he's simply going to sit in the place which has become the place he belongs, a place where he is closest to being happy, no, pleased he never moved, pleased to have this place paid for and not be running the Citgo in town chasing in circles regardless of the money, pleased to have the only station in the twelve miles of Route 21 between Garse and Corbett, nothing to look at across the street but trees rolling away toward Little Bear Mountain. Ruckelbar won't make fifty dollars the whole day and he simply leans back in the sunshine, pleased to have his tools put away and the bay swept and the office neat, just pleased to have the afternoon. As he sits and lifts his face to the old sun, he feels it and he's surprised that there is something else now, something new swimming underneath the ease he always feels at Bluestone, something about last night, and he tries to dismiss it but it will not be dismissed. It took years to achieve this separate peace and now something is coming undone.

Last night Ruckelbar had gone to Clare's room. After Marjorie had finished her pie and left the kitchen, her dishes on the table still, he'd sat as their talk played again in his head, burning there like a mistake. He hadn't known the Morton girl and in defending her he'd let his wife be injured. But he felt good about it somehow, that he had protested, and his mind had opened in the realization that something in him had been killed when they'd changed Marjorie's name, and he'd hated himself for not protesting then, but he knew too that he'd always just gone along. He lifted the two plates from the table and then put them down where they were. He went to Marjorie where she talked on the phone in the den and he stood before her until she put her palm over the speaker and said, annoyed, "What?" He said, "Get off the phone and go put your dishes away. Now." He said it in such a way that she spoke quickly into the telephone and hung up. Before she could rise, he added, "I think you should watch your language around your mother; I'm sure you didn't please her tonight in speaking so freely. She's worked hard to raise you correctly and you disappointed her."

"You started it," Marjorie said.

"Stop," he said. "You apologize to her tomorrow. It will mean a lot to her. You're everything she's got." Ruckelbar wanted to touch his daughter, put his hand on her cheek, but he didn't move, and in a moment Marjorie left the room. He had not done it too many times to reach out now, and besides, his hands, he always knew, were never really clean.

Ruckelbar went upstairs and knocked at his wife's door and then, surprising himself, went into the dark room. She was in bed and he sat beside her, but could do no more. He knew she was awake and he willed himself to put his arm around her, but he could not, pulling his fists up instead to his face and smelling in his knuckles all the scents of Bluestone.

IN THE EARLY AFTERNOON, a Chevy Two convertible pulls in to the gas pumps. At first Ruckelbar thinks it is two nuns, but when the two women get out laughing in their full black dresses, he sees they are gotten up as witches. One puts her tall black hat on and pulls a broom from the backseat ready to mug for any passing cars. Ruckelbar steps over. The bareheaded witch is switching on the pump. "Let me get that for you," he offers. "You'll smell like gasoline at your party."

"Great," the girl says. They are both about his daughter's age. "What are you going to be?" she asks him.

"This is it," Ruckelbar says, indicating his gray overall.

"Okay," the other witch says, "so what are you, the Prisoner of Bluestone?" They laugh and Ruckelbar has to laugh there in the sunshine. Girls. His daughter would not believe that he laughed with these girls; there'd be no way to explain it to her. The valve clicks off and he replaces the nozzle. As he does, the broom witch takes it from him and holds it as if to gas the broom.

"This, get this," she says. "Let's get out your camera, Paul." She's read his name in the patch. The other witch has grabbed her broom now and poses with her friend. Hearing his name and their laughter elates him and without hesitation, as if he'd planned it, he ducks into the station and retrieves the Nikon camera. He takes their picture there, two tall witches in the sunshine, and as he does, a passing car honks a salute. One of the witches steps out now seeing the bright blue station as if for the first time and says, "What is this, a movie set? I love it that you actually sell gas." She throws her broom and hat back into the car. The other girl, the driver, reaches deep into her costume, here and there, to find her money. She has some difficulty. Her hat falls off and Ruckelbar holds it for her, finally exchanging it for the nine dollars she pays him.

"Happy Halloween," she says, getting into the car. "I like your outfit. I hope they come to let you out someday."

The other girl has been at the car's radio and a song that Ruckelbar seems to remember rises around them. As the girls begin to pull away, she calls, "You can use that picture in your advertising!" And she throws him a flamboyant kiss.

All day long the traffic is desultory, five cars an hour pass Bluestone, the sound they make on Route 21 is a sound Ruckelbar knows by heart. He knows the trucks from the cars and he knows the high whine of the school buses. He knows if someone is speeding and he can tell if a car's intention is to slow and turn in. Just before sunset he hears that sound and a little white Ford Escort coasts into the gravel yard of the station, parking to one side. There is something odd about it and Ruckelbar thinks it is more costumes, two people, one wrapped like the Mummy, but then he sees it is a rental, and when the man and the woman get out and the man has the head bandage, he knows it is the owners of the Dodge van come to get whatever they'd left inside. People come the week after an accident and get their stuff. He stands and waves at the young people and then goes to unlock the chainlink gate, trying not to look at the man's head, which is swollen crazily over the unbandaged eye.

The woman strides directly for the van as Ruckelbar says, "Take your time, I don't close until six. No rush."

The woman calls from where she's slid open the side door of the van, "Bring the basket, Jerry. It's in the back."

So now it's Ruckelbar bending into the little Ford and extracting a huge plastic laundry basket because the man Jerry says he's not supposed to bend over until the swelling subsides in a week. "I have to sleep sitting up." Jerry's about thirty, his skull absolutely out of whack, a wrong-way oval, the skin on his exposed forehead about to split, shiny and yellow. Ruckelbar can smell the varnish of liquor on his breath. When he pulls the basket from the small backseat to hand it to Jerry, the young man has already wandered out back.

Ruckelbar takes the basket around to the open side of the van and offers it there, but the woman is on her knees on the middle seat bent into the far back, trying to untangle the straps of a collapsed child seat. Her cotton shift is drawn up so that her bare thighs are visible to him. Her underpants are a shiny satin blue and the configuration of her white thighs and the way they meet in the blue fabric seem a disembodied mystery to Ruckelbar. Ruckelbar looks away and steps back onto the moist yellow grid of grass where the Saab sat for eight weeks. He can hear the woman now, a soft sucking, and he knows she is weeping. He sets the basket there in the twilight and he walks back to the office. He is lit and shaken; he feels as he did when the witch said his name. On his way he hears Jerry break the mirror assembly from the van door and he turns to watch the young man throw it into the woods and then spin to the ground and grab his head.

Out front the sun is gone, the day is gone, it feels nothing but late. The daylight seems used, thin, good for nothing. He carries his chair back into the office and there in the new gloom is the boy, arms folded, leaning against the counter.

"You scared me," Ruckelbar says. "Hello." He sets the chair behind his steel desk and switches on the office fluorescents. He's lost for a moment and simply adds, "How are you?"

"Where's my sister's car?" the boy asks. He looks different close like this in the flat light; he's taller and younger, his pale face run with freckles. He's wearing a red plaid shirt unbuttoned over a faded black T-shirt.

"The insurance company came and got it. It was theirs." The boy takes this in and makes a face that says he understands. "Remember, I told you about this a couple of weeks ago?" The boy nods at him and then turns to the big window and looks out. His eyes are roaming and Ruckelbar sees the desperation.

The camera sits on the old steel desk, and in a second Ruckelbar decides what to do; if the boy recognizes it, he'll give it to him. Otherwise, he'll let this sleeping dog be. It feels like a good decision, but Ruckelbar is floating in a new world, he can tell. They can hear the loud voices outside, the man and the woman in the back, and Ruckelbar switches on the exterior lights.

"Where would the insurance take that car?"

"I don't know," Ruckelbar says.

"Would they fix it?"

"Probably part it out," Ruckelbar says. "They don't fix them anymore, many of them."

"It had been a good car for Sheila," the boy says. "Better than any of her friends had."

"I hear good things about the Saab," Ruckelbar says. "You want a Coke, something, candy bar?"

"I don't know why I'm out here now," the boy says. Their reflections have come up in the big windows. Ruckelbar drops quarters in the round-shouldered soda machine, another throwback, and opens the door for the boy to choose. "Root beer," the boy says, extracting the bottle.

"You live in Garse?" Ruckelbar asks him.

"Yeah," the boy says. His eyes are still wide, darting, and Ruckelbar can see the rim of moisture. The world outside is now set still on the pivot point of light, the glow of the station lights running into the air out over the road through the trees all the way to the even wash of silver along the horizon of Little Bear Mountain, and above the mountain like two huge ghosts floats the mirror image of the two of them. The leaves lie still. Standing by the door Ruckelbar can feel the air falling from the dark heavens, a faint chill falling from infinity. Tomorrow night it will be dark an hour earlier.

Now Ruckelbar hears the woman's voice from outside, around the building, a cry of some sort, and then the rental Escort does a short circle in the gravel in front of the Sunoco pumps and rips dust into the new dusk as it mounts Route 21 headed for Corbett. Ruckelbar and the boy have stepped outside. They watch the car disappear, turning on its lights after a few seconds on the pavement.

"There's a bonfire at the quarry tonight," Ruckelbar says. "Garse does it. You going?"

"We'd have gone with Sheila. She liked that stuff; she liked Halloween." The boy follows him back inside.

"You want a ride home?" Ruckelbar says, knowing instantly that it is the wrong thing to say, the offer of sympathy battering the boy over the brink, and now the boy stands crying stiffly, chin down, his arms crossed tighter than anything in the world.

Ruckelbar's heart heaves; he knows about this, about living in his silent house where a kind word would have broken him.

They stand that way, as if after an explosion, not knowing what to do; all the surprises in the room have been used up. Everything that happens now will be work. Ruckelbar is particularly out of ideas; he's not used to having anyone in the office for longer than it takes to make change. His father sometimes sat in here and chewed the fat with his cronies, DiPaulo and others, but Ruckelbar has never done it. He doesn't have any cronies. Now he doesn't know what to do. Ruckelbar points at the boy. "You go ahead, get the truck, bring it around front." He hands the boy his keys. The boy looks at him, so he goes on. "It's all right. You do it. You know my truck." With it dark now, Ruckelbar can see himself in the front window, a man in overalls. He's scared. It feels like something else could happen. He reaches for the phone and calls Clare, which he doesn't do three times a year. "Clare," he says, "I'm bringing somebody home who needs a warm meal. We're coming. It's not something we can talk over. We'll be about fifteen minutes, okay, honey? Did you hear me? Can you put on some of your tea?" He has never said anything like this to Clare in his life. The only people who are ever in their house are Clare's sister every other year and a few of Marjorie's friends who stand in the entry a minute or two.

"Paul," she says, and his name again jolts Ruckelbar. She goes on, "Marjorie spoke to me."

"I'm glad for that, Clare."

"She's a good girl, Paul."

"Yes, she is."

There is a pause and then Clare adds the last. "She misses her father. She said that today." Ruckelbar draws a quick breath and sees his truck like a ghost ship drift up front in the window. He lifts a hand to the boy in the truck. What he sees is a figure caught in the old yellow glass, a man in there. Ruckelbar thought everything was settled so long ago.

He turns off the light before he can see what the image will do, and he grabs his keys and the camera. Outside, the boy has slid to the passenger side. When Ruckelbar climbs in the boy says, in a new voice, easy and relaxed, "Nice truck. It's in good shape."

"It's a '62," Ruckelbar says. "My dad's truck. If you park them inside and change the oil every twenty-five hundred miles, they keep." He puts the camera on the seat. "This was in your sister's car."

The boy picks it up. "Cool," he says, hefting it. "This is a weird place," the boy says. "Who painted it blue?"

Ruckelbar is now in gear on the hardtop of Route 21. He looks back at Bluestone once, a little building in the dark. "My father did," he says.

ZANDUCE AT SECOND

BY HIS THIRTY-THIRD BIRTHDAY, a gray May day which found him having a warm cup of spice tea on the terrace of the Bay-side Inn in Annapolis, Maryland, with Carol Ann Menager, a nineteen-year-old woman he had hired out of the Bethesda Hilton Turntable Lounge at eleven o'clock that morning, Eddie Zanduce had killed eleven people and had that reputation, was famous for killing people, really the most famous killer of the day, his photograph in the sports section every week or so and somewhere in the article the phrase "eleven people" or "eleven fatalities"—in fact, the word *eleven* now had that association first, the number of the dead—and in all the major league baseball parks his full name could be heard every game day in some comment, the gist of which would be "Popcorn and beer for ten-fifty, that's bad, but just be glad Eddie Zanduce isn't here, for he'd kill you for sure," and the vendors would slide the beer across the counter and say, "Watch out for Eddie," which had come to supplant "Here you go," or "Have a nice day," in conversations even away from the parks. Everywhere he was that famous. Even this young woman, who has been working out of the Hilton for the past eight months not reading the papers and only watching as much TV. as one might watch in rented rooms in the early afternoon or late evening, not really news hours, even she knows his name, though she can't remember why she knows it and she finally asks him, her brow a furrow, "Eddie Zanduce? Are you on television? An actor?" And he smiles, raising the room-service teacup, but it's not a real smile. It is the placeholder expression he's been using for four years now since he first hit a baseball into the stands and it struck and killed a college sophomore, a young man, the papers were quick to point out, who was a straight-A student majoring in chemistry, and it is the kind of smile that makes him look nothing but old, a person who has seen it all and is now waiting for it all to be over. And in his old man's way he is patient thrugh the next part, a talk he has had with many people all around the country, letting them know that he is simply Eddie Zanduce, the third baseman for the Orioles who has killed several people with foul balls. It has been a pernicious series of accidents really, though he won't say that.

She already knows she's not there for sex, after an hour she can tell by the manner, the face, and he has a beautiful actor's face which has been stunned with a kind of ruin by his bad luck and the weight of bearing responsibility for what he has done as an athlete. He's in the second thousand afternoons of this new life and the loneliness seems to have a physical gravity; he's hired her because it would have been impossible not to. He's hired her to survive the afternoon.

The day has been a walk through the tony shopping district in Annapolis, where he has bought her a red cotton sweater with tortiseshell buttons. It is a perfect sweater for May, and it looks wonderful as she holds it before her; she has short brunette hair, shiny as a schoolgirl's, which he realizes she may be. Then a walk along the pier, just a walk, no talking. She doesn't because he doesn't, and early on such outings, she always follows the man's lead. Later, the fresh salad lunch from room service and the tea. She explores the suite, poking her head into the bright bathroom, the nicest bathroom in any hotel she's been in during her brief career. There's a hair dryer, a robe, a fridge, and a phone. The shower is also a steamroom and the tub is a vast marble dish. There is a little city of lotions and shampoos. She smiles and he says, Please, feel free. Then he lies on the bed while she showers and dresses; he likes to watch her dress, but that too is different because he lies there imagining a family scene, the young wife busy with her grooming, not immodest in her nakedness, her undergarments on the bed like something sweet and familiar. The tea was her idea when he told her she could have anything at all; and she saw he was one of the odd ones, there were so many odd ones anymore willing to pay for something she's never fully understood, and she's taken the not understanding as just being part of it, her job, men and women, life. She's known lots of people who didn't understand what they were doing; her parents, for example. Her decision to go to work this way was based on her vision of simply fucking men for money, but the months have been more wearing than she could have foreseen with all the chatter and the posturing, some men who only want to mope or weep all through their massage, others who want to walk ahead of her into two or three nightspots and then yell at her later in some bedroom at the Embassy Suites, too many who want her to tell them about some other bastard who has abused her or broken her heart. But here this Eddie Zanduce just drinks his tea with his old man's smile as he watches the stormy summer weather as if it were a home movie. They've been through it all already and he has said simply without pretension. No, that's all right. We won't be doing that, but you can shower later. I'll have you in town by five-thirty.

THE ELEVEN PEOPLE Eddie Zanduce has killed have been properly eulogized, the irony in the demise of each celebrated in the tabloid press, the potentials of their lives properly inflated, and their fame—brief though it may have been—certainly far beyond any which might have accompanied their natural passing, and so they needn't be listed here and made flesh again. They each float in the head of Eddie Zanduce in his every movement, though he has never said so, or acknowledged his burden in any public way, and it has become a kind of poor form now even in the press corps, a group not known for any form, good or bad, to bring it up. After the seventh person, a girl of nine who had gone with her four cousins to see the Orioles play New York over a year ago, and was removed from all earthly joy and worry by Eddie Zanduce's powerhouse line drive pulled foul into the seats behind third, the sportswriters dropped the whole story, letting it fall on page one of the second section: news. And even now after games, the five or six reporters who bother to come into the clubhouse—the Orioles are having a lackluster start, and have all but relinquished even a shot at the pennant—give Eddie Zanduce's locker a wide berth. Through it all, he has said one thing only, and that eleven times: "I'm sorry; this is terrible." When asked after the third fatality, a retired school principal who was unable to see and avoid the sharp shot of one of Eddie

Zanduce's foul balls, if the unfortunate accidents might make him consider leaving the game, he said, "No."

And he became so stoic in the eyes of the press and they painted him that way that there was a general wonder at how he could stand it having the eleven innocent people dead by his hand and they said things like "It would be hard on me" and "I couldn't take it." And so they marveled darkly at his ability to appear in his uniform, take the field at all, dive right when the hit required it and glove the ball, scrambling to his knees in time to make the throw either to first or to second if there was a chance for a double play. They noted that his batting slump worsened, and now he's gone weeks in the new season without a hit, but he plays because he's steady in the field and he can fill the stands. His face was the object of great scrutiny for expression, a scowl or a grin, because much could have been made of such a look. And when he was at the plate, standing in the box awaiting the pitch, his bat held rigid and ready off his right shoulder as if for business, this business and nothing else, the cameras went in on his face, his eyes, which were simply inscrutable to the nation of baseball fans.

And now, at thirty-three he lies on the queen-size bed of the Bayside Inn, his fingers twined behind his head, as he watches Carol Ann Menager come dripping into the room, her hair partially in a towel, her nineteen-year-old body a rose-and-pale pattern of the female form, five years away from any visible wear and tear from the vocation she has chosen. She warms him appearing this way, naked and ready to chat as she reaches for her lavender bra and puts it of all her clothing on first, simply as convenience, and the sight of her there bare and comfortable makes him feel the thing he has been missing: befriended.

"But you feel bad about it, right?" Carol Ann says. "It must hurt you to know what has happened."

"I do," he says, "I do. I feel as badly about it all as I should."

And now Carol Ann stops briefly, one leg in her lavender panties, and now she quickly pulls them up and says, "I don't know what you mean."

"I only mean what I said and nothing more," Eddie Zanduce says.

"What was the worst?"

He still reclines and answers: "They are all equally bad."

"The little girl?"

Eddie Zanduce draws a deep breath there on the bed and then speaks: "The little girl, whose name was Victoria Tuttle, and the tourist from Austria, whose name was Heinrich Vence, and the Toronto Blue Jay, a man in a costume named William Dirsk, who was standing on the home dugout when my line drive broke his sternum. And the eight others all equally unlikely and horrible, all equally bad. In fact, eleven isn't really worse than one for me, because I maxed out on one. It doesn't double with two. My capacity for such feelings, I found out, is limited. And I am full."

Carol Ann Menager sits on the bed and buttons her new sweater. There is no hurry in her actions. She is thinking. "And if you killed someone tonight?"

Here Eddie Zanduce turns to her, his head rolling in the cradle of his hands, and smiles the smile he's been using all day, though it hasn't worn thin. "I wouldn't like that," he says. "Although it has been shown to me that I am fully capable of such a thing."

"Is it bad luck to talk about?"

"I don't believe in luck, bad or good." He warms his smile

one more time for her and says, "I'm glad you came today. I wouldn't have ordered the tea." He swings his legs to sit up. "And the sweater, well, it looks very nice. We'll drive back when you're ready."

ON THE DRIVE NORTH Carol Ann Menager says one thing that stays with Eddie Zanduce after he drops her at her little blue Geo in the Hilton parking lot and after he has dressed and played three innings of baseball before a crowd of twenty-four thousand, the stadium a third full under low clouds this early in the season with the Orioles going ho-hum and school not out yet, and she says it like so much she has said in the six hours he has known her—right out of the blue as they cruise north from Annapolis on Route 2 in his thick silver Mercedes, a car he thinks nothing of and can afford not to think of, under the low sullen skies that bless and begrudge the very springtime hedgerows the car speeds past. It had all come to her as she'd assembled herself an hour before; and it is so different from what she's imagined, in fact, she'd paused while drying herself with the lush towel in the Bayside Inn, her foot on the edge of the tub, and she'd looked at the ceiling where a heavy raft of clouds crossed the domed skylight, and one hand on the towel against herself, she'd seen Eddie Zanduce so differently than she had thought. For one thing he wasn't married and playing the dark game that some men did, putting themselves closer and closer to the edge of their lives until something went over, and he wasn't simply off, the men who tried to own her for the three hundred dollars and then didn't touch her, and he wasn't cruel in the other more overt ways, nor was he turned so tight that to enjoy a cup of tea over the marina with a hooker was anything sexual, nor was she young enough to be his daughter, just none of it, but she could see that he had made his pact with the random killings he initiated at the plate in baseball parks and the agreement left him nothing but the long series of empty afternoons.

"You want to know why I became a hooker?" she asks.

"Not really," he says. He drives the way other men drive when there are things on their minds, but his mind, she knows, has but one thing in it—eleven times. "You have your reasons. I respect them. I think you should be careful and do what you choose."

"You didn't even see me," she says. "You don't even know who's in the car with you."

He doesn't answer. He says. "I'll have you back by five-thirty."

"A lot of men want to know why I would do such a thing. They call me young and beautiful and talented and ready for the world and many other things that any person in any walk of life would take as a compliment. And I make it my challenge, the only one after survive, to answer them all differently. Are you listening?"

Eddie Zanduce drives.

"Some of them I tell that I hate the work but enjoy the money; they like that because—to a man—it's true of them. Some I tell I love the work and would do it for free; and they like that because they're all boys. Everybody else gets a complicated story with a mother and a father and a boyfriend or two, sometimes an ex-husband, sometimes a child who is sometimes a girl and sometimes a boy, and we end up nodding over our coffees or our brandies or whatever we're talking over, and we smile at the wisdom of time, because there is nothing else to do but for them to agree with me or simply hear and nod and then smile, I do tell good stories, and that smile is the same smile you've been giving yourself all day. If you had your life figured out any better than I do, it would have been a different day back at your sailboat motel. Sorry to go on, because it doesn't matter, but I'll tell you the truth; what can it hurt, right? You're a killer. I'm just a whore. I'm a whore because I don't care, and because I don't care it's a perfect job. I don't see anybody else doing any better. Show me somebody who's got a grip, just one person. Survive. That's my motto. And then tell stories. What should I do, trot out to the community college and prepare for my future as a medical doctor? I don't think so."

Eddie Zanduce looks at the young woman. Her eyes are deeper, darker, near tears. "You are beautiful," he says. "I'm sorry if the day wasn't to your liking."

She has been treated one hundred ways, but not this way, not with this delicate diffidence, and she is surprised that it stings. She's been hurt and neglected and ignored and made to feel invisible, but this is different, somehow this is personal. "The day was fine. I just wish you'd seen me."

For some reason, Eddie Zanduce responds to this: "I don't see people. It's not what I do. I can't afford it." Having said it, he immediately regrets how true it sounds to him. Why is he talking to her? "I'm tired," he adds, and he is tired—of it all. He regrets his decision to have company, purchase it, because it has turned out to be what he wanted so long, and something about this girl has crossed into his view. She is smart and pretty and—he hates this—he does feel bad she's a hooker.

And then she says the haunting thing, the advice that he will carry into the game later that night. "Why don't you try to do it?" He looks at her as she finishes. "You've killed these people on accident. What if you tried? Could you kill somebody on purpose?"

At five twenty-five after driving the last forty minutes in a silence like the silence in the center of the rolling earth, Eddie Zanduce pulls into the Hilton lot and Carol Ann Menager says, "Right up there." When he stops the car, she steps out and says to him, "I'll be at the game. Thanks for the tea."

AND NOW at two and one, a count he loves, Eddie Zanduce steps out of the box, self-conscious in a way he hasn't been for years and years and can't figure out until he ticks upon it: she's here somewhere, taking the night off to catch a baseball game or else with a trick who even now would be charmed by her unaffected love for a night in the park, the two of them laughing like teenagers over popcorn, and now she'd be pointing down at Eddie, saying, "There, that's the guy." Eddie Zanduce listens to the low murmur of twenty-four thousand people who have chosen to attend tonight's game knowing he would be here, here at bat, which was a place from which he could harm them irreparably, for he has done it eleven times before. The announcers have handled it the same after the fourth death, a young lawyer taken by a hooked line shot, the ball shattering his occipital bone the final beat in a scene he'd watched every moment of from the tock! of the bat—when the ball was so small, a dot which grew through its unreliable one-second arc into a huge white spheroid of five ounces entering his face, and what the announcers began to say then was some version of "Please be alert, ladies and gentlemen, coming to the ballpark implies responsibility. That ball is likely to go absolutely anywhere." But everybody knows this. Every single soul, even the twenty Japanese businessmen not five days out of Osaka know about Eddie Zanduce, and their boxes behind first base titter and moan, even the four babies in arms not one of them five months old spread throughout the house know about the killer at the plate, as do the people sitting behind the babies disgusted at the parents for risking such a thing, and the drunks, a dozen people swimming that abyss as Eddie taps his cleats, they know, even one in his stuporous sleep, his head collapsed on his chest as if offering it up, knows that Eddie could kill any one of them tonight. The number eleven hovers everywhere as does the number twelve waiting to be written. It is already printed on   best-selling T-shirt, and there are others, "I'll be 12th," and "Take Me 12th!" and "NEXT," and many others, all on T-shirts which Eddie Zanduce could read in any crowd in any city in which the Orioles took the field. When he played baseball, when he was listed on the starting roster—where he'd been for seven years—the crowd was doubled. People came as they'd come out tonight on a chilly cloudy night in Baltimore, a night that should have seen ten thousand maybe, more likely eight, they flocked to the ballpark, crammed themselves into sold-out games or sat out—as tonight—in questionable weather as if they were asking to be twelfth, as if their lives were fully worthy of being interrupted, as if—like right now with Eddie stepping back into the batter's box—they were asking, Take me next, hit me, I have come here to be killed.

Eddie Zanduce remembers Carol Ann Menager in the car. He hoists his bat and says, "I'm going to kill one of you now."

"What's that, Eddie?"

Caulkins, the Minnesota catcher, has heard his threat, but it means nothing to Eddie, and he says that: "Nothing. Just something I'm going to do." He says this stepping back into the batter's box and lifts his bat up to the ready. Things are in place. And as if enacting the foretold, he slices the first pitch, savagely shaving it short into the first-base seats, the kind of ugly truncated liner that has only damage as its intent, and adrenaline pricks the twenty-four thousand hearts sitting in that dangerous circle, but after a beat that allows the gasp to subside, a catch-breath really that is merely overture for a scream, two young men in blue Maryland sweatshirts leap above the crowd there above first base and one waves his old brown mitt in which it is clear there is a baseball. They hug and hop up and down for a moment as the crowd witnesses it all sitting silent as the members of a scared congregation and then a roar begins which is like laughter in church and it rides on the night air, filling the stadium.

"I'll be damned," Caulkins declares, standing mask off behind Eddie Zanduce. "He caught that ball, Eddie."

Those words are etched in Eddie Zanduce's mind as he steps again up to the plate. He caught the ball. He looks across at the young men but they have sat down, dissolved, leaving a girl standing behind them in a red sweater who smiles at him widely and rises once on her toes and waves a little wave that says, "I knew it. I just knew it." She is alone standing there waving. Eddie thinks that: she's come alone.

The next pitch comes in fat and high and as Eddie Zanduce swings and connects he pictures this ball streaming down the line uninterrupted, too fast to be caught, a flash off the cranium of a man draining his beer at the very second a plate of bone carves into his brain and the lights go out. The real ball though snaps on a sharp hop over the third baseman, staying in fair territory for a double. Eddie Zanduce stands on second. There is a great cheering; he may be a killer but he is on the home team and he's driven in the first run of the ballgame. His first hit in this month of May. And Eddie Zanduce has a feeling he hasn't had for four years since it all began, since the weather in his life changed for good, and what he feels is anger. He can taste the dry anger in his mouth and it tastes good. He smiles and he knows the cameras are on him but he can't help himself he is so pleased to be angry, and the view he has now of the crowd behind the plate, three tiers of them, lifts him to a new feeling that he locks on in a second: he hates them. He hates them all so much that the rich feeling floods through his brain like nectar and his smile wants to close his eyes. He is transported by hatred, exulted, drenched. He leads off second, so on edge and pissed off he feels he's going to fly with this intoxicating hatred, and he smiles that different smile, the challenge and the glee, and he feels his heart beating in his neck and arms, hot here in the center of the world. It's a feeling you'd like to explain to someone after the game. He plans to. He's got two more at bats tonight, the gall rises in his throat like life itself, and he is going to kill somebody—or let them know he was trying.

THE HOUSE GOES UP

As you can see, I've got a nice body. But you can't get a house to go up with just a body. Other women think it's a body. I can't tell you how many times I've heard about it. They think it's just some sex thing. And sex is part of it, but if it was just having a good body, I couldn't even get them to sell the station wagon. So I've got this nice body and I take care of it in ways most women don't, but getting the house to go up is simpler than you'll ever know. It's got everything to do with men, how easy men are, how absolutely wide-eyed and pleased with themselves they are; how ripe to fall in love.

Men are simple. If you even knew what blank tablets they are, even the ones married ten, twelve years. In fact these guys are sometimes the simplest, the worst. You'd think they had not been out of the house at night for years or seen a woman in a public place, such as the Castaway, which is where they see me.

There they are, boys in men's clothing. Some guy has lived in the same house with a woman for years, and what he knows about women can best be described as zero. I'm not saying I don't take advantage of this. I work with the materials at hand, I admit it. What am I supposed to do, make it hard on myself? Just because it's easy doesn't mean it's not worth doing. I'm going to be—in many ways—their first woman.

So I wear this lace. The lace in their household is long gone, believe me, and I wear this camisole, something none of them have ever seen, even the lawyers. They weren't really looking until they met me. And they like this: a skirt, zipper in the back. How exotic! And a blouse like this: silk, French cuffs. I mean, they don't understand these things. It is so easy. By the time they've lit your cigarette, by the time they've moved one barstool down from their friend who is also appraising you carefully, you can sense the house ready to move. I wear simple, understated jewelry, these are tiny zirconium, kind of classy, and I don't wear a necklace with this blouse. Gaudy jewelry is not necessary. Neither is cleavage. Not at all. And, I've got cleavage. I could show them a cleavage, but if I did that, if I hypnotized them with grand curves that started them scratching their palms, the house would never even quiver. They'd take charge and do the stupid things men do to get something they want. Cleavage is no good; men understand cleavage. It won't work at all.

The same with tight jeans. Why would you do that? To show them something they can have? Men understand tight jeans. As the woman said, cleavage is cleavage, coming or going. It's as simple as the man himself. What you need is mystery. My rule is three layers. I wear three layers: everywhere.

This is not about sex, do you see? This is about real estate. This is about getting someone's attention. This is about making him think that it's all his idea, which actually will happen as easily as rain falls, and eventually he'll be in love . . . and the rest will follow.

When I was married, we lived not far from here really, on a funky little street that dead-ended into a golf course, and my husband, who I understood less then than I do now, laid a flag-stone patio and lined it with a short and pretty flagstone wall. It was a place to have cocktails in the afternoons and we did that for a few years. It was good, or so I thought at the time, and now I see that it was neither bad nor good. It was something we did out of doors. It was different from drinking at the Castaway.

In the Castaway I do very little. I sit at the bar for an hour and then I sit alone at a little table near the bar for the rest of the night. I drink Wallbangers or Sunrises or Sombreros, drinks the men are not going to drink, drinks they don't understand. Sometimes I smoke and sometimes I don't smoke. I keep my cigarettes in this. It's not really silver, but they've never even seen a cigarette case before. I say very little and smile shyly. They like it if I seem hurt somehow as if the last man in my life was a beast, a cretin, a rude rotten son of a bitch, and though I never use those words all I have to do is nod quietly and eventually the men will. They are all heroes ready to show me—if I will allow it—that men can be decent, caring individuals. "That son of a bitch," they'll say. "Didn't he understand anything?" And then they'll order me another drink once I tell them what I'm drink-ing, and we'll grin about how different that is from their Miller Lite or Seagram's and Seven, and it's a moment I love and try to extend any way I can, this man at my table, his hand in the air like a man, making an order for a woman he is in the process of saving. And though he won't make a move that night or offer his number or his card—if he has one—or ask for mine or really stay at the table when his friend at the bar signals that it is time to go, when I look up at him for the last time, keeping my head down, our eyes will meet and I will see it: the house is going up.

Of course he'll know where to find me the next Thursday night, same table. This time he'll come alone and we'll have a heart-to-heart; rather, he'll have a heart-to-heart and it will be all so high school, him leaning over the table, his eyes moist, meaning every word: the big things he'd always wanted to do, I mean not just drivers, even if he's a judge or a chemist, the things he's been kept from, the tragedy of time, of compromise, of—really—marriage. I'll listen without moving. It's terrifically poignant, let me tell you. Once in a while a song will come on the jukebox, "Stand by Your Man," or "Fools' Parade," and I'll sigh and let him know that the music has affected me, and I'll see the look in his eyes triple. Eventually he'll fall silent having said more to me in two hours than he's said in years and then he'll ask if I want to dance. I'll shake my head. The line: I'm not a girl who really dances. You should see him swell to hear this. Then, depending on my mood—if I'm up for hurrying things— I'll ask if it's okay if we get out of here. "I mean, could we just sit in your car for a while?"

Once you've sat in his car, it's a done deal. He'll want to do something. What I let him do is kiss me once and then I shake that off and hold his hand in both of mine. No one has done that for him in years. You hold a man's hand in both of your hands for ten minutes and he'll love you forever. That is what love is. I sit there and hint, faintly, at how hard things are for me, but how optimistic I am about tomorrow, and then I'll kiss him quickly on the cheek and get out of his car and into mine and drive home.

The rest is rote. I'll send him a note—to his office—during

the week thanking him for taking the time to talk to me, to share his feelings, saying that his being open meant so much to me. His wife isn't writing him notes anymore and he'll call and want to see me right away. And it's funny, but when you do see him, it won't be sex. I either bring him here or we go to a motel, and either way, there'll be a lot of pacing. The sudden charge of being alone in private will drive him mad. He'll want to dive for me, but he respects me too much, and besides, he's my savior, my hero. See how simple it all is, how simple men are? Oh, we'll end up in a clinch, again some agony right out of high school, where he'll get a couple of layers past the slip or camisole in ab-solute wonderland at such things, all that lace, and him so steamed up, he'll never get to skin. It's so goofy, him standing up quickly and tucking in his shirt, and me on the bed propped up on one arm, and now I'll show him a little cleavage, and I'll look as serious as I ever have looked serious and I'll try to smile, but what I'll say is: "I want to see you again. I need you. No, never mind, go on, go home. I'll be all right." By this time he will have come over to the bed and I'll level with him. "I'm a girl who doesn't do this," I'll say. "But I want you again. All of you. I feel so funny, but: *I need it.*"

And so it goes. You'll give him some little presents and he'll buy you a couple of expensive things that make you wonder, a thousand-dollar watch and a real nice Walkman, and you'll teach him new sex tricks for a month or two until his wife finds out. It always takes the wife longer than I planned. Where is that girl? But oddly enough, it won't matter to my guy, because, you see, he loves me. He's not up for five bad scenes and ten months of therapy. This marriage is over. Kids and all. So much for Fido, the tennis club, every single thing that has kept him from being all he could be.

This is a tricky period for me. I'll tell him that we'd better not see each other for a while; it's only good sense. He'll take a room somewhere and call me five times a day. I feel guilty, I'll say. I'm confused. Meanwhile, I'll cruise his neighborhood waiting for the moment which got me into this whole deal. I mean, I'm happy all the while, I'm happy right now, I'm naturally a happy person, but I'm not really happy happy until I see the FOR SALE sign stabbed into the front lawn.

The house goes up. They have to deal with the realty, some tired schoolteacher, dry as old bread and dumb as a stick, and they have to think: seven percent. This stranger who can't speak grammatical English—a person who must have bored her classes to death for years without end in social studies—is going to get seven percent of our house.

And then they have to divide the possessions, think about all the stuff they've brought into the house for years and years— it goes miles beyond the stereo and houseplants; there are roomsful.

Later, six, ten weeks, after I've let him know that there is no way I can continue with him, that to be a "homewrecker" is more than I can bear and that I'm sure he's better off without me—I am, after all, just a damaged soul floating through the universe. After he's history, I'll drive by his house again. Sometimes I'll go by the garage sale; there she is, the wife, with four aisles of their lives spread in the sun. She won't know me. Maybe I'll buy something, a little wall mirror or a little hibachi for the terrace. If there's a box of tapes, I'll buy a cassette or two for my new Walkman.

I don't gloat. I do what I do. But I get a rush in these weeks, the aftermath. I love to drive by and just read the FOR SALE sign again. On the dry days of fall, it swings sometimes in the wind and I slow to hear the creaking. A healthy tuft of grass grows around the post like a hairy halo. The house is now empty, and the whole yard takes on a dusty, wild look, vacant. It could use a little water, but, of course, the mower, a red Toro with a grass catcher, that's long gone. That will never cut this grass again.

And between men sometimes I simply drive, float the neighborhoods at twilight before I go to the bar, and I admire the smooth blue lawns shimmering under the wheezing evening sprinklers and I watch the yellow squares of windows light against the night, maybe a porch lamp will illuminate a flagstone terrace. I love that. Flagstone. There is nothing that speaks of marriage more than well-laid flagstone and a short stone wall. I drive slowly past these formidable homes and I see the FOR SALE signs on every block. There is nothing, not even flagstone, that can prevent a house from going up.

II

"Well, sir, what do you suggest:

we stand here and shed tears

and call each other names?

Or shall we go to Istanbul?"

Sydney Greenstreet as Caspar Gutman
in *The Maltese Falcon*

WHAT WE WANTED TO DO

WHAT WE WANTED to do was spill boiling oil onto the heads of our enemies as they attempted to bang down the gates of our village, but, as everyone now knows, we had some problems, primarily technical problems, that prevented us from doing what we wanted to do the way we had hoped to do it. What we're asking for today is another chance.

There has been so much media attention to this boiling oil issue that it is time to clear the air. There is a great deal of pressure to dismantle the system we have in place and bring the oil down off the roof. Even though there isn't much left. This would be a mistake. Yes, there were problems last month during the Visigoth raid, but as I will note, these are easily remedied.

From its inception I have been intimately involved in the boiling oil project—research, development, physical deployment. I also happened to be team leader on the roof last month when we had occasion to try the system during the Visigoth attack, about which so much has been written.

(It was not an "entirely successful" sortie, as I will show. The Visigoths, about two dozen, did penetrate the city and rape and plunder for several hours, but *there was no pillaging.* And make no questions about it—they now know we have oil on the roof and several of them are going to think twice before battering down our door again. I'm not saying it may not happen, but when it does, they know we'll be ready.)

First, the very concept of oil on the roof upset so many of our villagers. Granted, it is exotic, but all great ideas seem strange at first. When our researchers realized we could position a cauldron two hundred feet directly above our main portals, they began to see the possibilities of the greatest strategic defense system in the history of mankind.

The cauldron was expensive. We all knew a good defense was going to be costly. The cauldron was manufactured locally after procuring copper and brass from our mines, and it took—as is common knowledge—two years to complete. It is a beautiful thing capable of holding one hundred and ten gallons of oil. What we could not foresee was the expense and delay of building an armature. Well, of course, it's not enough to have a big pot, pretty at it may be; how are you going to pour its hot contents on your enemies? The construction of an adequate superstructure for the apparatus required dear time: another year during which the Huns and the Exogoths were raiding our village almost weekly. Let me ask you to remember that era—was that any fun?

I want to emphasize that we were committed to this program—and we remain committed. But at every turn we've met problems that our researchers could not—regardless of their intelligence and intuition—have foreseen. For instance: how were we to get a nineteen-hundred-pound brass cauldron onto the roof? When had such a question been asked before? And at each of these impossible challenges, our boiling oil teams have come up with solutions. The cauldron was raised to the roof by means of a custom-designed net and hoist including a rope four inches in diameter which was woven on the spot under less than ideal conditions as the Retrogoths and the Niligoths plundered our village almost incessantly during the cauldron's four-month ascent. To our great and everlasting credit, we did not drop the pot. The superstructure for the pouring device was dropped once, but it was easily repaired on-site, two hundred feet above the village steps.

That was quite a moment, and I remember it well. Standing on the roof by that gleaming symbol of our impending safety, a bright brass (and a few lesser metals) beacon to the world that we were not going to take it anymore. The wind carried up to us the cries of villagers being carried away by either the Maxigoths or the Minigoths, it was hard to tell. But there we stood, and as I felt the wind in my hair and watched the sporadic procession of home furnishings being carried out of our violated gates, I knew we were perched on the edge of a new epoch.

Well, there was some excitement; we began at once. We started a fire under the cauldron and knew we would all soon be safe. At that point I made a mistake, which I now readily admit. In the utter ebullience of the moment I called down—I did not "scream maniacally" as was reported—I called down that *it would not be long,* and I probably shouldn't have, because it may have led some of our citizenry to lower their guard. It was a mistake. I admit it. There were, as we found out almost immediately, still some bugs to be worked out of the program. For instance, there had never been a fire on top of the entry tower before, and yes, as everyone is aware, we had to spend more time than we really wanted containing the blaze, fueled as it was by the fresh high winds and the tower's wooden shingles. But I hasten to add that the damage was moderate, as moderate as a four-hour fire could be, and the billowing black smoke surely gave further intruders lurking in the hills pause as they considered finding any spoils in our ashes!

But throughout this relentless series of setbacks, pitfalls, and rooftop fires, there has been a hard core of us absolutely dedicated to doing what we wanted to do, and that was to splash scalding oil onto intruders as they pried or battered yet again at our old damaged gates. To us a little fire on the rooftop was of no consequence, a fribble, a tiny obstacle to be stepped over with an easy stride. Were we tired? Were we dirty? Were some of us burned and cranky? No matter! We were committed. And so the next day, the first quiet day we'd had in this village in months, that same sooty cadre stood in the warm ashes high above the entry steps and tried again. We knew—as we know right now—that our enemies are manifold and voracious and generally rude and persistent, and we wanted to be ready.

But tell me this: where does one find out how soon before an enemy attack to put the oil on to boil? Does anyone know? Let me assure you it is not in any book! We were writing the book!

We were vigilant. We squinted at the horizon all day long. And when we first saw the dust in the foothills we refired our cauldron, using wood which had been elevated through the night in woven baskets. Even speaking about it here today, I can feel the excitement stirring in my heart. The orange flames licked the sides of the brass container hungrily as if in concert with our own desperate desire for security and revenge. In the distance I could see the phalanx of Visigoths marching toward us like a warship through a sea of dust, and in my soul I pitied them and the end toward which they so steadfastly hastened. They seemed the very incarnation of mistake, their dreams of a day abusing our friends and families and of petty arsony and lewd public behavior about to be extinguished in one gorgeous wash of searing oil! I was beside myself.

It is important to know now that everyone on the roof that day exhibited orderly and methodical behavior. There was professional conduct of the first magnitude. There was no wild screaming or cursing or even the kind of sarcastic chuckling which you might expect in those about to enjoy a well-deserved and long-delayed victory. The problems of the day were not attributable to inappropriate deportment. My staff was good. It was when the Visigoths had approached close enough that we could see their cruel eyes and we could read the savage and misspelled tattoos that I realized our error. At that time I put my hand on the smooth side of our beautiful cauldron and found it only vaguely warm. Lukewarm. Tepid.

We had not known then what we now know. *We need to put the oil on sooner.*

It was my decision and my decision alone to do what we did, and that was to pour the warm oil on our enemies as they milled about the front gates, hammering at it with their truncheons.

Now this is where my report diverges from so many of the popular accounts. We have heard it said that the warm oil served as a stimulant to the attack that followed, the attack I alluded to earlier in which the criminal activity seemed even more animated than usual in the minds of some of our townspeople. Let me say first: I was an eyewitness. I gave the order to pour the oil and I witnessed its descent. I am happy and proud to report that the oil hit its target with an accuracy and completeness I could have only dreamed of. We got them all. There was oil everywhere. We soaked them, we coated them, we covered them in a lustrous layer of oil. Unfortunately, as everyone knows, it was only warm. Their immediate reaction was also what I had hoped for: surprise and panic. This, however, lasted about one second. Then several of them looked up into my face and began waving their fists in what I could only take as a tribute. And then, yes, they did become quite agitated anew, recommencing their assault on the weary planks of our patchwork gates. Some have said that they were on the verge of abandoning their attack before the oil was cast upon them, which I assure you is not true.

As to the attack that followed, it was no different in magnitude or intensity from any of the dozens we suffer every year. It may have seemed more odd or extreme since the perpetrators were greasy and thereby more offensive, and they did take every stick of furniture left in the village, including the pews from the church, every chair in the great hall, and four milking stools, the last four, from the dairy.

But I for one am simply tired of hearing about the slippery stain on the village steps. Yes, there is a bit of a mess, and yes, some of it seems to be permanent. My team removed what they could with salt and talc all this week. All I'll say now is watch your step as you come and go; in my mind it's a small inconvenience to pay for a perfect weapon system.

So, we've had our trial run. We gathered a lot of data. And you all know we'll be ready next time. We are going to get to do what we wanted to do. We will vex and repel our enemies with boiling oil. In the meantime, who needs furniture? We have a project! We need the determination not to lose the dream, and we need a lot of firewood. They will come again. You know it and I know it, and let's simply commit ourselves to making sure that the oil, when it falls, is very hot.

THE CHROMIUM HOOK

JACK CRAMBLE

Everybody knows this, that we pulled in the driveway and I found the hook when I went around to Jill's door. It was caught in the door handle, hanging there like I don't know what. I didn't know what it was at first, but when Jill got out she knew, and she started screaming, for which I don't blame her. Her father came out and made like where had we been and did we know it was almost one o'clock. He's a good guy, but under real pressure, I guess, since his wife had her troubles. Anyway, he looks at the hook, and then he looks Jill over real good, suspicious-like, like we'd been up to something, which we definitely had not. We had been, as everybody knows, up at Conversation Point with our debate files, and the time got away from us. I was helping her with her arguments, asking questions, like that, things like "What are the drawbacks of an international nuclear-test-ban treaty?" And she would fish around in her file

box and try to find the answer. Her one shot at college is the debate team, and their big meet with Northwoods was a week
from that Saturday. It was Mr. Royaltuber who called the police,
and the word got out.

JILL ROYALTUBER

IT WAS THE scaredest I've ever been, and when I think of how
close that homicidal maniac came to getting us and doing whatever he was going to do with that big vicious hook, my blood
runs cold. Jack was really brave. He wanted to get out of the car
after we heard the first noises, the scrapings, and see what it was,
but I wouldn't let him. Sometimes boys just don't have any
sense. We'd already heard about the escaped homicidal maniac
on the radio. They'd interrupted *Wild Johnny Hateras's Top
Twenty Country Countdown* with the news bulletin that some
one-armed madman had escaped the loony bin on Demon Hill
and was sort of armed and dangerous. And of course Discussion
Point is right there by the iron fence of the nuthouse. We had
gone up to Discussion Point to work through some problems I'd
been having since my mom left, and Jack was talking to me
about being strong and saying he'd be there for me and not to
get too depressed and to look on the sunny side of things, that
Mom was better off in the hospital—she certainly seemed hap-
pier. So Jack was being that thing, supportive, which I love. A
boyfriend who is captain of football is one thing, and a boyfriend
who is captain of football and supportive is another. But I kept
him from getting out of the car after we heard the noises. The
wind had come up a little and it was dark as dark, and I said,
"Let's just get out of here." Jack wasn't afraid. He wanted to
stay. But I told him it was late, and then we heard the scratching

closer, against the car, and it felt like it was right on my bare spine. "Pull out!" I yelled, and he gunned the engine of his Ford—it's a wonderful car, which he did all the work on—and we headed for home.

DR. STEWART NARKENPIE, DIRECTOR, THE SPINARD PSYCHIATRIC INSTITUTE

IT IS NOT a loony bin. It is not a nuthouse or a funny farm. It's not even an insane asylum. It is, as I've been telling everyone in this community for the twenty-two years I've lived here, the Spinard Psychiatric Institute, a center for the treatment of psychological disorders. It is a medical hospital, the building and grounds of which occupy just under two hundred acres on the top of Decatur Hill, and it employs thirty-eight citizens from the lovely town of Griggs, including Mr. Howard Lugdrum, who was injured seriously in last week's incident. I have spoken to the Rotary Club once a year for forever, as well as to the Lions and the Elks and the Junior Achievement and the graduating class of the high school and the Vocational Outreach in the Griggs Middle School, explaining what we do and how we do it and that the Spinard Psychiatric Institute is not a loony bin or any other kind of bin, and I am not getting through. It is not a bin! Even though a large portion of our community has had family and friends enter the Institute as patients only to be returned to the community after treatment in better shape than before, and even though most everybody has visited the grounds—if not for personal reasons, then certainly at our annual Community Picnic on the South Lawn—there still persists this incurable sense that once you pass under the Spinard stone arch you are entering the twilight zone. Yes, we do have a big iron fence, because some of our patients get confused and could possibly wander away, and yes, the buildings, some of them, have bars over the windows for the safety of our patients, and some of our patients wear restraints when out-of-doors, but they are dangerous to no one but themselves. I cannot say how weary I am of setting the record straight. It is not a nuthouse, and I am not a mad scientist. We don't have any mad scientists, mad professors, or mad doctors. No one's mad. We don't use that term. We do have some disturbed patients, but we're treating them, and there is a chance—with rest counseling, and medication—that they will get better. We do not perform operations except as they become medically necessary. We had an appendectomy last fall. We do not operate on the brain. We do not—as the high school paper suggests regularly—do brain transplants, dissections, or enlargements. Most recently I had to speak with Wild Johnny Hateras at KGRG, the radio station in Griggs, about the prank news bulletin on Halloween, which is just the kind of thing that keeps any understanding between the Institute and the town in tatters and is responsible, I think, for the harm resulting from last Saturday's incident, about which we've heard so much.

MR. HOWARD LUGDRUM

IT HURT. DON'T you think that hurt? Everybody talks about the kids: oh, they were scared, they were frightened and nervous, oh, they were terrified. Well, think about it—had two trespassers yanked off *their* prosthesis? In the course of doing their job, were either of *them* pulled from their feet and dragged till an arm came off, and left there tumbling in the dirt? As it turns out, I was lucky I was wearing my simple hook and the straps broke; if I'd been wearing my regular armature, those two little criminals would have dragged me to death, and we'd have murder here instead of reckless endangerment.

ROD BUDDAROCK

IF ANYBODY, ONE person, says anything, one thing, about my buddy Jack Cramble being up there at Passion Point to do anything, one thing, besides help little Jill Royaltuber with family problems, such as they are, I'll find that person and use his lying butt to wipe up Main Street. I'm not joking here. I know Jack from being co-captain of football, and I know what I'm saying. Of course, he could have come to the team party out at the Landing, but here was a girl who had some troubles and he was there to help. There's been a lot of talk about what they were really doing. Jack made that crack about debate, which was too bad, because he couldn't get within two miles of the debate team—I'm a better debater than Jack and Jill put together—but he only said that to protect Jill's reputation, such as it is. She's a nice girl, but a little confused. It was only last year that her mom went bonkers, and Jill herself went a little nuts about that time, but she is no slut. If anybody, one person, says anything about Jill Royaltuber being a wide-mouthed, round-heeled slut, I'll find that person and trouble will certainly rain down upon his or her head like hot shit from Mars.

MR. HOWARD LUGDRUM

I'D SEEN THE car before. It's a two-door Ford, blue-and-white. There are five or six cars I see there by our north fence in the pine grove. They bring their girlfriends up from town in the good weather, and we find the empty beer bottles and condoms. The kids call it Passion Point. We had a timed light system there until a few years ago, but the Environmental Protection Agency asked us to dismantle it because of the Weaver's bat, a protected species that hunts there at night. The deal about the parking is that the grove is our property and we stand liable for any harm. Two kids climb in the backseat of some old clunker with a faulty exhaust and the Institute would be sued until the thirteenth of never. I mean, these are kids at night in old cars. What we've done is put the grove on the watchman's tour, and one of us takes the big flashlight and shines it on a few bare butts every night of the week. Until last week, it's been kind of funny—I mean, you see some white rear end hop up, and then the cars start up and wheel out like scurrying rats. Once interrupted, they don't come back. Until the next night. Like I said, these are kids.

I'm in charge of the buildings and grounds at the Institute, and I like my work there; it's been a good place to me.

SHERIFF CURTIS MANSARACK

THE MOST FREQUENTLY asked question is "When you bust a beer bust, do you keep the beer?" For Pete's sake. Every weekend I roust one or two of these high school beer parties, most often on the hill or down at Ander's Landing. Sometimes, though, there'll be a complaint and I'll be called to a private residence. A lot of these kids know me by now, and they know that about eleven-thirty old Sheriff Mansarack will slip up in his cruiser and flash the lights long enough for every drunk sophomore to run into the bushes so that I can cite the two or three seniors too drunk to flee.

I was in the middle of such a raid last Saturday night, Halloween, a night when I know for a sure fact that there is going to be trouble, and I got the call from Oleena Weenz, our dispatcher. There had been, in her words, a "vicious assault by a pervert," and she directed me to the address on Eider Street where I found Mr. Rick Royaltuber and the two young people and heard the story. I knew the boy, Jack Cramble, and had seen him play football earlier that night when Griggs beat Bark City, and I was kind of surprised that he wasn't down with the rest of the team drinking beer at the Landing. I also knew Mr. Royaltuber, as I had taken the call when his wife went off the deep end a year ago. When a guy helps you subdue his wife and pries her fingers off a rusty pair of kitchen scissors while you hold her kicking and screaming on your lap on the front porch in front of all the neighborhood, you remember him. That was a bad deal, embarrassing for me to get caught off guard. I mean, she looked normal. I hadn't seen the scissors. And it was bad for old Royaltuber too, with her shrieking out about him porking what's-her-name, the wife of old Dr. Dizzy up at the loony bin, and rattling those scissors at us. Hey, sometimes kitchen tools are the worst. And she was strong.

Anyway, I spoke to Mr. Royaltuber and I saw the hook there on the car door. It was a regular artificial arm, straps and all, one of them torn, and it scared me too. I mean, when that thing came off, it had to hurt. I took the report, but it wasn't all in line, and to tell the truth neither was the front of the Royaltuber girl's shirt. She was misbuttoned the way you are after putting away your playthings in a hurry.

The Cramble boy kept at me to get back up there right away before the pervert got somebody else, saying things like Wasn't I the sheriff? Wasn't I supposed to do something? Well, I could see *he* wanted to do something, something that had been interrupted up at Passion Point, so I just told them all it was going to be all right, which it was, and I headed back to the Landing, where I was able to run off about ten kids and confiscate a case and a half of Castle Moat, which is not my favorite, but it'll do.

MR. HOWARD LUGDRUM

I NEVER MARRIED. Years ago, after my accident, I changed my plans about a career in tennis and went up to college near Brippert and got into their vocational-ed program in hotel management.

I was pretty numbed out after Cassie's family moved who knows where. This is a long time ago now. Her girlfriend Maggie Rayne hung around with me for a while, and then I think she saw the limits of a man with one hand and moved on. Her father was a professor at the medical school, and I was clearly outclassed. So, anyway, I never married. I didn't realize the torch was still lit—or really how alive I could feel—until I saw Cassie again a year ago, when she was carried up here kicking and screaming, spitting and cursing, her eyes red and her hair wild, the most beautiful thing I've seen in, let's see, seventeen years.

MRS. MARGARET RAYNE NARKENPIE

I HAD NOT planned on a mountaintop in Bushville. I had not actually thought I would—after seven years of graduate study and three years at the Highborn Academy—find myself banished to the left-hand districts of Forsaken Acres, dressing for dinner at the macaroni-and-cheese outlet, opting for the creamed tuna on special nights. I had lived in a wasteland as a girl, and I thought I was through with it. Let's just say, for the sake of argument, that marrying the highest-ranking doctor in my father's finest class, a tall, good-looking psychiatrist of sterling promise who could have written his ticket anywhere in the civilized world, I was expecting to live in a place where there was more than one Quicky Freeze and a Video Hut. I had dared to think London, New York, even Albuquerque. I had not imagined Griggs. My husband—who has his Institute and his staff and his many duties and all his important vision for psychiatric health care—can't even see Griggs. So, the way I live here and whom I associate with in this outpost of desolation is, it would seem to me, my business.

Mr. Royaltuber handles all the television and monitor maintenance and repair for the Spinard Institute. He has also helped us with the satellite dish and the cable connections we use at home. He's a nice man, and I have lunch with him from time to time. We've become, under the circumstances and in this barren place, friends. I met his wife only once, when I was at his home. It was less than pleasant.

MR. WILD JOHNNY HATERAS,
RADIO PERSONALITY, KGRG

IF ANYBODY PRETENDS to be hurt or surprised by our little prank, they're bad actors. Everybody in this burg knows what we do on Halloween with the "important news bulletin" and the hook. We've been doing it since I started spinning platters here twelve years ago. Nick goes out and slips a dozen of the phony hooks on car doors, and then I interrupt the program with my announcement about the maniac. I think of it as our little annual contribution to birth control, all those kids jumping up when I cut into "Unchained Melody" with my homicide-and-hook news brief. When we started, we used those plastic hooks from the costume shop in Orpenhook, but, sad to say, gang, it's impossible to scare anybody anymore with a plastic hook. Don't tell *me* the world's a better place. So now we get them in Bark City, little steel hooks that at least look authentic for a few minutes. But this will probably be the last year we send Nick out with anything at all, because of the trouble up by the nuthouse, and because he's afraid of getting shot. Can you believe that? You go out on Halloween to have a little fun anymore and you run a good chance of getting plugged? Hey, Griggs, wake up, all is not well. If you can't harass the teenagers without running the risk of getting killed, this town is in trouble.

MRS. CASSIE ROYALTUBER

IT'S FUNNY WHAT people think. You try to put a pair of kitchen scissors in the doctor's wife one afternoon and they think (a) you're crazy, or (b) you're desperately in love with your sweet husband, or (c) you caught her in bed with your husband, with whom she's been sleeping for two years, and therefore you're just slow to catch on, since everybody, absolutely everybody else in this village, which is not exactly full of geniuses, has known about the affair since the first week, or (d) that you're all three: crazy, in love, and slow to catch on.

Well, it is simply exhilarating to be liberated from (a) the slings and (b) the arrows of public opinion and to take it for what it is, which is (a) irrelevant and (b) as absolutely wrong as it can be.

Who in their right mind—which is where I find myself— would consider that the television repairman's wife might have another reason? Who would grant the past its due, the vast sweeping privilege of history and justice? Who would guess that (a) I knew Mrs. Narkenpie before she and her doctor moved to Griggs, in fact before she was Mrs. Narkenpie, when she was simply Margaret Rayne, and that (b) she was the prime reason I had been forcibly removed from my one true love so many years ago, and that (c) I had chosen those scissors not for the convenience of their being right there in the drawer but because they were appropriate—I wanted to cut her the way she cut my Howard.

And the things I screamed I screamed on purpose. How are you going to get into the loony bin unless they think you're loony?

ROD BUDDAROCK

WHAT HE DOES is take the beer. This seems to be his only deal as a cop, to drive around on weekends and take beer from kids. And he keeps the beer. Some kids just go ahead and buy his brand, which is the Rocary Red Ale—fifteen dollars a case at any Ale and Mail. Isn't there any crime to stop? How do you get a job like that—free car and free beer? Hey, I'll sign up. As is, I'm glad I'm a senior and out of here next spring. He comes into our Halloween party last Saturday, the same night that there's a maniac with a hook roaming all over Griggs, attacking kids, slashing at everything in sight, and he busts us, scaring everybody shitless and causing Ardeen Roster to break her nose running away in the bushes, and he writes *me* a ticket for it. Then, while some monster with one arm has practically taken over the whole town, he takes our beer, and there's still about three and a half cases of Red Pelican—which you have to drive to Orpenhook to even find—so I'm forced to live the rest of my life picturing this civic wart pounding down our Pelicans every afternoon on his deck while he dreams up his next law enforcement strategy. Life is hard on the young, man, count on it.

MR. HOWARD LUGDRUM

I'M GOING TO NEED to get my hook back. There's a lot of work up here that requires two hands. We've got leaves to rake, tons, and a lot of other seasonal preventive maintenance—storm windows, snowplow prep work—and I can't load and deliver firewood effectively without my prosthesis. I'd appreciate its return as soon as possible.

MR. RICK ROYALTUBER

CASSIE WAS NEVER even cranky all these years. I mean, of all people, she's the last I'd expect to crack up. It was tough to send her off. It hurt me to put her up on the hill, but there it was, we couldn't deny she'd lost control of her senses when she tried to harm Mrs. Narkenpie. How do you think I feel knowing she's up there, locked up in a nuthouse night and day, wearing a straitjacket or what-have-you. But the doctor said it was for the best, and I believe him. These things, so many of them, are beyond ordinary folks.

SHERIFF CURTIS MANSARACK

INCIDENTAL TO MY call on the Royaltubers Halloween night, I had the Cramble boy pop open his trunk, and I found the following:

nylon rope, 100 yards
hammer
hatchet
power screwdriver
small grappling hook
duct tape, two rolls
canvas, 12x12
flashlights, two
pepper spray, two canisters
bolt cutters
Doritos, large bag, taco-flavored

JILL ROYALTUBER

I NEVER SAW his face. I never saw anything really. All I heard
was some vibrations, I guess—maybe footsteps in the leaves, and
then a kind of metallic clicking like scritch, scritch, and I was
begging Jack to pull out, to just pull out of there. We hadn't
been doing anything. Jack had hurt his hand in the game against
Bark City, and I had been massaging that. We were trying to
relax.

MRS. CASSIE ROYALTUBER

I LOVED HOWARD from Moment Number One, when we met
seventeen years ago, on the night of the construction of our high
school's homecoming float, which was a big ram. We were the
Cragview Rams. He and I were part of the tissue brigade, two
dozen kids handing Kleenex each to each in a line that ended at
the chicken-wire sculpture, which slowly filled with the red,
white, and blue paper. He was standing next to me and our

hands touched once a second as the tissue flowed through us, my left hand, his right hand, which he would lose that spring, touch, touch, touch. He was the first tender boy I ever knew, and I was happy when he invited me to the homecoming dance. There is no need to explain every delicate step of that fall, Moment Number Two and Moment Number Three, except to say that when we gave our hearts, we gave our hearts completely, and everything else followed. It was the year I died and went to heaven for a while.

Moment Number Four I discovered that I was pregnant, and even that seemed magical, until my father found out thanks to my jealous classmate, wicked Maggie Rayne, who also told him that Howard and I always met after school in the Knopdish junkyard. And it was there, Moment Number Five, that my father found us in the rear seat of an old VW van, which had been like a haven for us, and he yanked me out onto the ground and slammed that rusty door forever, or so I thought, on my one good thing—Howard Lugdrum.

Howard, I heard, lost his arm in the "accident," and my father moved us far away, here to Griggs. The Moments now go unnumbered. Before the summer was over, young, handsome Ricky Royaltuber was coming round, and I didn't care, I did my part. I wasn't even there, and I guess I've been away a long time.

I didn't care when Maggie Rayne moved to town with her fancy doctor, and I didn't care that she went after and got Ricky. It freed me in a way. I can hardly remember who came and went in our house—Jill's friends, neighbors, boys.

But when I heard that the stars had relented and uncrossed and again lined up my way, that Howard had come to Griggs, working at this very loony bin in which I now live, I woke up, and in a major way. Afternoons, he comes in with a cup of tea, and we sit and he lets me hold it while we talk. These days are sweet days again, full of sweet moments. Even now I can see him through these bars, cleaning the windows of the van with the big circles of his left hand.

JACK CRAMBLE

I DON'T CARE who knows it now: I was going to spring her. Last year, when I was a nobody from nowhere, she was the only person in town who would listen. I was the new kid in town then, not captain of the football team, and she was always there for me. I told her everything. It was easier and better than talking to my own folks, and she was different, a woman, more woman than anybody I'll ever meet again. I loved her and I loved the way she talked, putting my problems in perspective a, b, c, or 1, 2, 3. To keep seeing her I started dating that dipweed Jill, who has been nothing but a pain in the neck with all her "sharing," "caring," and "daring." Such a girl. Such a needy little girl. Just thinking about her makes my skin crawl. Let's go up to the Point, she'd say, so she could crawl all over me. I'll tell you flat, she knows nothing about being a real woman like her mother. We went up there on Halloween after the game so I could scope out the fence and the approach to Cassie's room. The plan was for midnight. Of course, Jill jumped me when we parked, and lucky for me the watchman came along or I'd have had to go all the way. As it was, her pants were already to her ankles, and he got a hell of a view of her bare ass in the window.

But it hasn't deterred me. Cassie and I are meant to be together, that's clear, regardless of the age difference. I'm going back up there in a night or two and busting her out. Football season's over, and it's time to be me. My heart knows what to do, and it says, Scale the wall, break her out!

MR. HOWARD LUGDRUM

SHE WAS HERE almost a year before she told me. Though I knew instantly we'd pick up where we left off, my heart steady through the years to the one woman I loved, Cassie waited to be sure it was still me, I guess, that a man with one arm could be trusted. So last week we were at tea in her room after her counseling session, and she looked at me funny and told me something amazing: I have a daughter! A daughter! Having Cassie back in my life after so long seemed almost too much for me to bear, and now . . . a child. Well, not a child but a young woman. And, Cassie told me, I could see her if I went by the north pine grove sometime after nine that night, Halloween. I'd see a blue-and-white Ford and my daughter would be in it! It was all I could do to get the afternoon hours out of the way; it was a waiting like no waiting I have ever known. My daughter! As it happened, I don't know if I saw her or not, just somebody's butt in the moonlight.

SHERIFF CURTIS MANSARACK

FALL IN GRIGGS is a good thing: the leaves change color and there's football and the smell of the first wood fires. Halloween's my last big chance to score a beer bust, and I almost never miss. I didn't miss this year. Every year there's a hook, sometimes more than one, and it takes a week or two for things to quiet down. I don't mind the hooks; the waxed windows are worse. I'd trade the waxed windows for two more hooks. Soon it will snow and life gets real easy: there's no cop better than old Jack Frost.

PERSON BEHIND LAST TREE IN THE TWILIGHT

AT NIGHT, AS I drift through these woods, I tap my hook from time to time against my leg and the feel of the hard iron spurs me on past fence and fern, past drooping branches and the cobbed underbrush. What I need is an older-model American car parked alone in the dark, one with a grip handle I can snare. The lift handles are no good, and everything anymore has the aerodynamic lift handles. I want a '60 Fairlane or a '58 Chevrolet, a car with bench seats big enough for two young people to get comfortable and tangle up their clothing and their brainwaves so that they forget the dark, the woods, the person with a hook, every Halloween, approaching through the leaves.

A NOTE
ON THE TYPE

No ALPHABET COMES along full-grown. A period of development is required for the individual letters to bloom and then another period for them to adjust to their place in the entire set,
and sometimes this period can be a few weeks or it can be a life-
time. No quality font maker ever sat down and wrote out A to Z
just like that. It doesn't happen. Getting Ray Bold right required
five months, these last five months, an intense creative period for
me which has included my ten-week escape from the state facilities at Windchime, Nevada, and my return here one week ago.
Though I have always continued sharpening my letters while
incarcerated, most of the real development of Ray Bold occurred
while I was on the outside, actively eluding the authorities.
There's a kind of energy in the out-of-doors, moving primarily
along the sides of things, always hungry, sleeping thinly in hard
places, that awakens in me the primal desire toward print.

And though Ray Bold is my best typeface and the culmination

of my work in the field, I should explain it is also my last—for the reasons this note on the type will illuminate. I started this whole thing in the first place because I had been given some time at the Fort Nippers Juvenile Facility in Colorado—two months for reckless endangerment, which is what they call Grand Theft Auto when you first start in at it, and I was rooming with Little Ricky Grudnaut, who had only just commenced his life as an arsonist by burning down all four barns in the nearby town of Ulna in a single night the previous February. Juvenile facilities, as you can imagine, are prime locations for meeting famous criminals early in their careers, and Little Ricky went on, as everyone now knows, to burn down eleven Chicken Gigundo Franchise outlets before he was apprehended on fire himself in Napkin, Oklahoma, and asked to be extinguished.

But impulsive and poultry-phobic as he may have become later, Little Ricky Grudnaut gave me some valuable advice so many years ago. I'd moped around our cell for a week—it was really a kind of dorm room—staring at this and that, and he looked up from the tattoo he was etching in his forearm with an old car key. It was Satan's head, he told me, and it was pretty red, but it only looked like some big face with real bad hair—and he said, "Look, Ray, get something to do or you'll lose it. Make something up." He threw me then my first instrument, a green golf pencil he'd had hidden in his shoe.

It was there in Fort Nippers, fresh from the brutality of my own household, that I began the doodling that would evolve into these many alphabets which I've used to measure each of my unauthorized sorties from state-sponsored facilities. Little Ricky Grudnaut saw my first R that day and was encouraging. "It ain't the devil," he said, "but it's a start."

I HAVE DECIDED to accept the offer of reduced charges for full disclosure of how and where I sustained my escape. In Windchime I had been sharing a cell with Bobby Lee Swinghammer, the boxer and public enemy, who had battered so many officials during his divorce proceedings last year in Carson City. Bobby Lee was not happy to have a lowly car thief in his cell and he had even less patience with my alphabets. I tried to explain to him that I wasn't simply a car thief, that I was now, in the words of the court, "an habitual criminal" (though my only crime had been to steal cars which I had been doing for years and years), and I tried to show him what I was working on with Ray Bold. Bobby Lee Swinghammer's comment was that it looked "piss plain," and it irked him so badly that he then showed me in the next few weeks some of his own lettercraft. These were primarily the initials *B* and *L* and *S* that he had worked on while on the telephone with his attorney. And they are perfect examples of what is wrong with any font that comes to life in prison.

The design is a result of too much time. I've seen them in every facility in which I have resided, these letters too cute to read, I mean flat-out baroque. Serifs on the *T*'s that weigh ten pounds, Bobby Lee had beaked serifs on his *S*'s that were big as shoes. His *B* was three dimensional, ten feet deep, a *B* you could move into, four rooms and a bath on the first floor alone. I mean he had all afternoon while his lawyer said "We'll see" a dozen different ways, why not do some gingerbread, some decoration? I kept my remarks to a minimum. But I've seen a lot of this, graffiti so ornate you couldn't find the letters in the words. And what all of that is about is one thing and it's *having time*. I respect it and I understand it—a lot of my colleagues have got plenty of time, and now I've got some again too, but it's a style that is just not for me.

I became a car thief because it seemed a quick and efficient way to get away from my father's fists, and I became a font maker because I was caught. After my very first arrest—I'd taken a red Firebird from in front of a 7-Eleven—in fact in my first alphabet, made with a golf pencil, I tried my hand at serification. I was thirteen and I didn't know any better. These were pretty letters. I mean, they had a kind of beauty. I filigreed the C's and G's and the Q until they looked like they were choking on lace. But what? They stood there these letters so tricked up you wouldn't take them out of the house, too much makeup, and you knew they weren't any good. For me, that is. You put a shadow line along the stem of an R and then beak the tail it's too heavy to move.

The initials that Bobby Lee Swinghammer had been carving into the back of his hand with a Motel 6 ballpoint pen looked like monuments. You could visit them, but they were going absolutely nowhere.

And that's what I wanted in this last one, Ray Bold, a font that says "movement." I mean, I was taking it with me and I was going to use it, essentially, on the run. Bobby Lee was right, it is plain but it can travel light.

I want to make it clear right here, though Bobby Lee and I had our differences and he did on occasion pummel me about the head and upper trunk (not as hard as he could have, god knows), he is not the reason I escaped from Windchime. I have escaped, as the documents point out, eleven times from various facilities throughout this part of the west, and it was never because of any individual cellmate, though Bobby Lee was one of the most animated I've encountered. I like him as a person and

I'm pleased that his appeal is being heard and that soon he will
be resuming his life as an athlete.

I walked out of Windchime because I had the chance. I found
that lab coat folded over the handrail on our stairs. Then,
dressed as a medical technician, with my hair parted right down
the middle, I walked out of there one afternoon, carrying a clipboard I'd made myself in shop, and which is I'll admit right here
the single most powerful accessory to any costume. You carry a
clipboard, they won't mess with you.

Anyway, that windy spring day I had no idea of the direction
this new alphabet would take. I knew I would begin writing;
everybody knew that. I always do it. I've been doing it for more
than twenty years. When my father backhanded me for the last
time I fled the place but not before making my *Ray* on his sedan
with the edge of a nickel. It wasn't great, and I don't care to
write with money as a rule, but it was me, my instinct for lettercraft at the very start.

I also knew I'd be spending plenty of time in the wilderness,
the high desert there around Windchime and the forests as they
reach into Idaho and the world beyond. I know now that, yes,
landscape did have a clear effect on the development of Ray
Bold, the broad clean vistas of Nevada, the residual chill those
first few April nights, and the sharp chunk of flint I selected to
inscribe my name on a stock tank near Popknock. That first *Ray*
showed many clues about the alphabet to come: the *R* (and the *R*
is very dear to me, of course) made in a single stroke (the stem
bolder than the tail); the small case *a*, unclosed; and the capital *Y,*
which resembles an *X.* These earmarks of early Ray Bold would
be repeated again and again in my travels—the single stroke, the
open letter, the imprecise armature. To me they all say one
thing: energy.

I made that *Ray* just about nightfall the second night, and I was fairly sure the shepherd might have seen me cross open ground from a rocky bluff to the tank, and so, writing there in the near dark on the heavily oxidized old steel tank while I knelt on the sharp stones and breathed hard from the run (I'd had little exercise at Windchime), I was scared and happy at once, which as anyone knows are the perfect conditions under which to write your name. *Ray.* It was a beginning.

"Why do it?" they say. "You want to be famous?" It is a question so wrongheaded that it kind of hurts. Because what I do, I do for myself. Most of the time you're out there in some dumpster behind the Royal Food in Triplet or you're sitting in a culvert in Marvin or in a boxcar on a siding in Old Delphi (all places I've been) and what you make, you better make for yourself. There aren't a whole lot of people going to come along and appreciate the understated loop on your *g* or the precision of any of your descenders. I mean, that's the way I figured it. When I fell into that dumpster in Triplet I was scratched and bleeding from hurrying with a barbed-wire fence, and I sat there on the old produce looking at the metal side of that bin, and then after I'd pried a tenpenny nail from a wooden melon crate I made my *Ray,* the best I knew how, knowing only I would see it. And in poor light. I made it for myself. It existed for a moment and then I heard the dogs and I was on the run again.

There was once a week later when I took that gray LeBaron in Marvin and it ran out of gas almost immediately, midtown, right opposite the Blue Ribbon Hardware, and I could see the town cop cruising up behind, and I took off on foot. And I can run when there's a reason, but as I run I always think, as I was thinking that day: where would I make my *Ray.* The two are linked with me: to run is to write. That day after about half a mile, I crawled into a canal duct, a square cement tube with about four inches of water running through the bottom. And with a round rock as big as a grapefruit sitting in that cold irrigation water, I did it there: *Ray*. It wasn't for the critics and it wasn't for the press. They wouldn't be along this way. It was for me. And it was as pure a *Ray* as I've ever done. I couldn't find that place today with a compass.

At times like that when you're in the heat of creation, making your mark, you don't think about hanging a hairline serif on the Y. It seems pretty plainly what it is: an indulgence. Form should fit function, the man said, and I'm with him.

After Marvin, that night in the water, I got sick and slept two or three days in hayfields near there. As everyone knows I moved from there to that Tuffshed I lived in near Shutout for a week getting my strength back. The reports had me eating dog food, and I'll just say to that I ate some *dog food,* dry food, I think it was Yumpup, but there were also lots of nuts and berries in the vicinity and I enjoyed them as well.

Everyone also knows about the three families I met and traveled with briefly. The German couple's story just appeared in *Der Spielplotz* and so most of Germany and Austria are familiar with me and my typeface. I hope that their tale doesn't prevent other Europeans from visiting Yellowstone and talking with Americans at the photo-vistas. I'm still amused that they thought I was a university professor (because I talked a little about my work), but on a three-state, five-month run from the law you're bound to be misunderstood. The two American families seemed to have no difficulty believing they'd fallen into the hands of an escaped felon, and though I did interrupt their vacations, I thought we all had a fine time, and I returned all of their equipment except the one blue windbreaker in good condition.

THOUGH I HAVE decided to tell my story, I don't see how it is going to help them catch the next guy. Because those last five weeks were not typical in the least. Fortunately, by the time I arrived in Sanction, Idaho, Ray Bold was mostly complete, for I lost interest in it for a while.

Walking through that town one evening, I took a blue Country Squire station wagon, the largest car I ever stole, from the gravel lot of the Farmers' Exchange. About a quarter mile later I discovered Mrs. Kathleen McKay in the back of the vehicle among her gear. When you find a woman in the car you're stealing, there is a good chance the law will view that as kidnapping, so when Mrs. McKay called out, "Now who is driving me home?" I answered, truthfully, "Just me, Ray." And at the four-way, when she said left, I turned left.

Now it is an odd thing to meet a widow in that way, and the month that followed, five weeks really, were odd too, and I'm just getting the handle on it now. Mrs. McKay's main interests were in painting pictures with oil paints and in fixing up the farm. Her place was 105 acres five miles out of Sanction and the house was very fine, being block and two stories with a steep metal snow roof. Her husband had farmed the little place, she said, but not very well. He had been a Mormon from a fine string of them, but he was a drinker and they'd had no children, and so the church, she said, had not been too sorry to let them go.

She told me all this while making my bed in the little out-building by the barn, and when she finished, she said, "Now I'm glad you're here, Ray. And I hope tomorrow you could help me repair the culvert."

I had thought it would be painting the barn, which was a grand building, faded but not peeling, or mowing the acres and acres of weeds, which I could see were full of rabbits. But no, it was replacing the culvert in the road to the house. It was generally collapsed along its length and rusted through in two big places. It was a hard crossing for any vehicle. Looking at it, I didn't really know where to start. I'd hid in plenty of culverts, mostly larger than this one, which was a thirty-inch corrugated-steel tube, but I'd never replaced one. The first thing, I started her old tractor, an International, and chained up to the ruined culvert and ripped it out of the ground like I don't know what. I mean, it was a satisfying start, and I'll just tell you right out, I was involved.

I trenched the throughway with a shovel, good work that took two days, and then I laid her shiny new culvert in there pretty as a piece of jewelry. I set it solid and then buried the thing and packed the road again so that there wasn't a hump, there wasn't a bump, there wasn't a ripple as you crossed. I spent an extra day dredging the ditch, but that was gilding the lily, and I was just showing off.

And you know what: she paid me with a pie. I'm not joking. I parked the tractor and hung up the shovel and on the way back to my room, she met me in the dooryard like some picture out of the *Farmer's Almanac,* which there were plenty of lying around, and she handed me an apple pie in a glass dish. It was warm and swollen up so the seams on the crosshatch piecrust were steaming.

Well, I don't know, but this was a little different period for old Ray. I already had this good feather bed in the old tack room and the smell of leather and the summer evenings and now I had had six days of good work where I had been the boss and I had a glass pie dish in my hands in the open air of Idaho. What I'm saying here is that I was affected. All of this had affected me.

To tell the truth, kindness was a new thing. My father was a crude man who never hesitated to push a child to the ground. As a cop in the town of Brown River he was not amused to have a son who was a thief. And my mother had more than she could handle with five kids and preferred to travel with the Red Cross from flood to fire across the plains. And so, all these years, I've been a loner and happy at it I thought, until Mrs. McKay showed me her apple pie. Such a surprise, that tenderness. I had heard of such things before, but I honestly didn't think I was the type.

I ate the pie and that affected me, two warm pieces, and then I ate a piece cool in the morning for breakfast along with Mrs. McKay's coffee sitting over her checked tablecloth in the main house as another day came up to get the world and I was affected further. I'm not making excuses, these are facts. When I stood up to go out and commence the mowing, Mrs. McKay said it could wait a couple of days. How'd she say it? Like this: "Ray, I believe that could wait a day or two."

And that was that. It was three days when I came out of that house again; it didn't really make any difference to those weeds. I moved into the main house. I can barely talk about it except to say these were decent days to me. I rode a tractor through the sunny fields of Idaho, mowing, slowing from time to time to let the rabbits run ahead of the blades. And in the evenings there was washing up and hot meals and Mrs. McKay. The whole time, I mean every minute of every day of all five weeks, I never made a *Ray*. And this is a place with all that barnwood and a metal silo. I didn't scratch a letter big or small, and there were plenty of good places. Do you hear me? I'd lost the desire.

But, in the meantime I was a farmer, I guess, or a hired hand, something. I did take an interest in Mrs. McKay's paintings, which were portraits, I suppose, portraits of farmers in shirt-sleeves and overalls, that kind of thing. They were good paintings in my opinion, I mean, you could tell what they were, and she had some twenty of the things on her sunporch, where she painted. She didn't paint any of the farmers' wives or animals or like that, but I could see her orange tractor in the back of three or four of the pictures. I like that, the real touches. A tractor way out behind some guy in a painting, say only three inches tall, adds a lot to it for me, especially when it is a tractor I know pretty well.

Mrs. McKay showed some of these portraits at the fair each year and had ribbons in her book. At night on that screen porch listening to the crickets and hearing the moths bump against the screens, I'd be sitting side by side with her looking at the scrapbook. I'd be tired and she would smell nice. I see now that I was in a kind of spell, as I said, I was affected. Times I sensed I was far gone, but could do nothing about it.

One night, for example, she turned to me in the bed and asked, "What is it you were in jail for, Ray? Were you a car thief?"

I wasn't even surprised by this and I answered with the truth, which is the way I've always answered questions. "Yes," I said. "I took a lot of cars. And I was caught for it."

"Why did you?"

"I took the first one to run away. I was young, a boy, and I liked having it, and as soon as I could I took another. And it became a habit for me. I've taken a lot of cars I didn't especially want or need. It's been my life in a way, right until the other week when I took your car, though I would have been just as pleased to walk or hitchhike." I had already told her that first day that I had been headed for Yellowstone National Park, though I didn't tell her I was planning on making Rays all over the damn place.

After a while that night in the bed she just said, "I see." And she said it sweetly, sleepily, and I took it for what it was.

WELL, THIS DREAM doesn't last long. Five weeks is just a minute, really, and things began to shift in the final days. For one thing I came to understand that I was the person Mrs. McKay was painting now by the fact of the cut fields in the background. The face wasn't right, but maybe that's okay, because my face isn't right. In real life it's a little thin, off-center. She'd corrected that, which is her privilege as an artist, and further she'd put a dreamy look on the guy's face, which I suppose is a real nod toward accuracy.

"Are these your other men?" I asked her one night after supper. We'd spoken frankly from the outset and there was no need to change now, even though I had uncomfortable feelings about her artwork; it affected me now by making me sad. And I knew what was going on though I could not help myself. I could not go out in the yard and steal her car again and pick up my plans where I'd dropped them. I'll say it because I know it was true, I was beyond affected, I was in love with Mrs. McKay. I could tell because I was just full of hard wonder, a feeling I understood was jealousy. I mean there were almost two dozen paintings out there on the porch.

But my question hit a wrong note. Mrs. McKay looked at me

while she figured out what I was asking and then her face kind
of folded and she went up to bed. I didn't think as it was happening to say I was sorry, though I was sorry in a second, sorrier
really for that remark than for any of the two hundred forty or
so vehicles I had taken, the inconvenience and damage that had
often accompanied their disappearance. What followed was my
worst night, I'd say. I'm a car thief and I am not used to hurting
people's feelings. If I hurt their feelings, I'm not usually there to
be part of it. And I cared for Mrs. McKay in a way that was
strange to me too. I sat there until sunrise when I printed a little
apology on a piece of paper, squaring the letters in a way that felt
quite odd, but they were legible, which is what I was after: "I'm
sorry for being a fool. Please forgive me. Love, Ray." I made the
Ray in cursive, something I've done only three or four times in
my whole life. Then I went out to paint the barn.

It was midmorning when I turned from where I stood high
on that ladder painting the barn and saw the sheriff's two vehicles where they were parked below me. I hadn't heard them because cars didn't make any whump-whump crossing that new
culvert. When I saw those two Fords, I thought it would come
back to me like a lost dog—the need to run and run, and make a
Ray around the first hard corner. But it didn't. I looked down
and saw the sheriff. There were two kids in the other car, county
deputies, and I descended the ladder and didn't spill a drop of
that paint. The sheriff greeted me by name and I greeted him
back. The men allowed me to seal the gallon of barn red and to
put my tools away. One of the kids helped me with the ladder.
None of them drew their sidearms and I appreciated that.

It was as they were cuffing me that Mrs. McKay came out.
She came right up and took my arm and the men stepped back
for a moment. I will always remember her face there, so serious

and pure. She said, "They were friends, Ray. Other men who have helped me keep this place together. I never gave any other man an apple pie, not even Mr. McKay." I loved her for saying that. She didn't have to. You have a woman make that kind of statement in broad daylight in front of the county officials and it's a bracing experience; it certainly braced me. I smiled there as happy as I'd been in this life. As the deputy helped me into the car I realized that for the first time *ever* I was leaving home. I'd never really had one before.

"Save that paint," I said to Mrs. McKay. "I'll be back and finish this job." I saw her face and it has sustained me.

THEY HAD FOUND me because I'd mowed. Think about it, you drive County Road 216 twice a week for a few years and then one day a hundred acres of milkweed, goldenrod, and what-have-you are trimmed like a city park. You'd make a phone call, which is what the sheriff had done. That's what change is, a clue.

So, HERE I AM in Windchime once again. I work at this second series of Ray Bold an hour or two a day. I can feel it evolving, that is, the font is a little more vertical than it was when I was on the outside and I'm thickening the stems. And I'm thinking it would look good with a spur serif—there's time. It doesn't have all the energy of Ray Bold I, but it's an alphabet with staying power, and it has a different purpose: it has to keep me busy for fifteen months, when I'll be going home to paint a barn and mow the fields. My days as a font maker are numbered.

My new cellmate, Victor Lee Peterson, the semifamous archer and survivalist who extorted all that money from Harrah's in

Reno recently and then put arrows in the radiators of so many state vehicles during his botched escape on horseback, has no time for my work. He leafs through the notebooks and shakes his head. He's spent three weeks now etching a target, five concentric circles on the wall, and I'll say this, he's got a steady hand and he's got a good understanding of symmetry. But, a target? He says the same thing about my letters. "The ABC's?" he said when he first saw my work. I smile at him. I kind of like him. He's an anarchist, but I think I can get through. As I said today: "Victor. You've got to treat it right. It's just the alphabet but sometimes it's all we've got."

III

If you haven't gambled for love in the moonlight,

then you haven't gambled at all.

—"The Moonlight Gambler,"
lyrics by Bob Hilliard, music by Phil Springer

NIGHTCAP

I WAS FILING deeds, or rather, I had been filing deeds all day, and now I was taking a break to rest my head on the corner of my walnut desk and moan, when there was a knock at my door. My heart kicked in. People don't come to my office. From time to time folders are slipped under my door, but my clients don't come here. They call me and I copy something and send it to them. I'm an attorney.

Still and all, I hadn't been much of anything since Lily, the woman I loved, had—justifiably—asked me to move out three months ago. Simply, these were days of filing. I didn't moan that often, but I sat still for hours—hours I couldn't bill to anyone. I wanted Lily back, and the short of it is that I'm not going to get her back in this story. She's not even *in* this story. There's another woman in this story, and I wish I could say there's another man. But there isn't. It's me.

And now the heavy golden doorknob turned, and the woman

entered. She wore a red print cowboy shirt and tight Levi's and under one arm she held a tiny maroon purse.

"Wrong room," I said. I had about four wrong rooms a week.

"Jack," she said, stepping forward. It was either not the wrong room or really the wrong room. "I'm Lynn LaMoine. Phyllis told me that if I came over there was a good chance I could talk you into going to the ball game tonight."

Well. She had me sitting down, half embarrassed about having my moaning interrupted, overheard, and her sister, Phyllis, Madame Cause-Effect, the most feared wrongful death attorney in the state, somehow knew that I was in limbo. I steered the middle road; it would be the last time. "I like baseball," I said. "But don't you have a husband?"

She nodded for a while, her mouth set. "Yeah," she said. "I was married, but . . . maybe you remember Clark Dewar?"

"Sure," I said. "He's at Stover-Reynolds."

She kept nodding. "A lawyer." Then she said the thing that sealed this small chapter of my cheap fate. "Look, I just thought it might be fun to sit outside in the night and watch the game. I'm not good at being lonely. And I don't like the lessons."

It was a page from my book, and I jumped right in. "We could go to the game," I told her. "The Gulls aren't very good, but I've got an old classmate who's coach, and the park organist is worth the price of admission."

At this she smiled so that just the tips of her front teeth showed and stood on one leg so that her shape in those Levi's cut a hard curve against the door behind her. I heard myself saying, "And the beer is cold and it's not going to rain." I explained that I didn't have a car and gave her my address. As a rule I try not to view women as their parts, but—as I said—my moaning had been interrupted and the whole era had me in a hammerlock, and as Lynn turned, her backside involuntarily brought to mind a raw word from some corner of my youth: tail.

THAT NIGHT as I eased into her car I realized that this was the first time I had been in a car alone with a woman for four weeks. For a moment, nine or ten seconds, it actually felt like a date. Ten tops. Though I hadn't accomplished anything with my life so far, I was showered and shined and the water in my hair was evaporating in a promising way, and we were going to the ball game.

I looked over at Lynn in her black silky skirt and plum sweater. She looked like a lot of women today: good. I couldn't tell if this was the outfit of a woman in deep physical need or not. The outfit didn't look overtly sexual, or maybe it did but so did everything else. And then I realized that in the muggy backwash late in this sour month, I felt the faint but unmistakable physical stir of desire. I've got to admit, it was a relief. I took it as a sign of well-being, possibly good health. It was a feeling that well-directed could get me somewhere.

As we arrived, turning onto Thirteenth South under the jutting cement bleachers of Derks Field, I smiled at myself for being so simple. I glanced again at Lynn's wardrobe. You can't tell a thing anymore by the way people dress; it only helps in court. No one dresses like a prostitute these days, not even the prostitutes. And besides, in my eight-year-old Sears khakis and blanched blue Oxford-cloth shirt from an era so far bygone only the Everly Brothers would have remembered it, I looked like the person in trouble, the person in deep, inarticulate need.

IN THE AMBIGUITY in which American ballparks exist, and they are a ragtag bunch, Derks Field is it. It is simply the loveliest garden of a small ballpark in the western United States. The stadium itself is primarily crumbling concrete poured the year I was born and named after John C. Derks, the sports editor at the *Tribune* who helped found the Pacific Coast League, Triple A Baseball, years ago. Though it could seat just over ten thousand, the average crowd these days was a scattered four hundred or so. This little Eden is situated, like most ballparks, in a kind of tough low-rent district spotted with small warehouses and storage yards for rusting heavy equipment.

As a boy I had come here and seen Dick Stuart play first base for the Bees; it was said he could hit the ball to Sugarhouse, which was about six miles into deep center. And my college team had played several games here my senior year while the campus field was being moved from behind the Medical School to Fort Douglas, and I mean Derks was a field that made you just want to take a few slides in the rich clay, dive for a liner in the lush grass.

Lynn and I parked in the back of the nearby All-Oil gas station and walked through a moderately threatening bevy of ten-year-old street kids milling outside the ticket office. When the game started, they would fan out across the street and wait to fight over foul balls, worth a buck apiece at the gate.

I love the moment of emerging into a baseball stadium, seeing all the new distance across the expanse of green grass made magical by the field lights bright in the incipient twilight. The bright cartoon colors on the ads of the home-run fence make a little carnival of their own, and above the "401 Feet" sign in straight-away center, the purple mountains of the Wasatch Front strike the sky, holding their stashes of snow like pink secrets in the last daylight.

I felt right at home. There was Midgely, the only guy who

stayed with baseball from our college squad, standing on the dugout steps just like a coach is supposed to look; there were all the teenage baseball wives sitting in the box behind the dugout, their blond hair buoyant in the fresh air, their babies struggling in the lap blankets; there was the empty box that our firm bought for the season and which no one *ever* used; there beyond first in the general admission were Benito Antenna's fans, a grouping of eight or nine of the largest women in the state come to cheer their true love; and there riding the summer air like the aroma of peanuts and popcorn and cut grass were the strains of Steiner Brightenbeeker's organ cutting a quirky and satanic version of "How Much Is That Doggie in the Window?" I could see the Phantom of the Ballpark himself pounding out the melody in his little green cell, way up at the top of the bleachers next to the press box.

"What?" Lynn said, returning from a solo venture underneath the bleachers. She handed me a beer and a bag of peanuts. She had insisted on buying the tickets, too. Evidently I was being hosted at the home park tonight.

"Nothing. That guy's an old friend of mine." I pointed up at Steiner. Lynn was being real nice, I guess, but I felt a little screwy. Seeing Steiner and being in a ballpark made me think for a minute the world might want me back. He had played at our parties.

And it is my custom with people I don't know to pay my own way, at least, but as she had handed me the plastic cup, I had accepted it without protest. My financial picture precluded many old customs, even those grounded on common sense. I would keep track and pay her back sometime. Besides, early in the game, so to speak, I didn't have the sense not to become indebted to this woman.

"Don't you want a beer?" I asked her. She demurred, and retrieved a flask of what turned out to be brandy from her purse along with a silver thimble. I don't have the official word on this, but I don't think you drink brandy at the ballpark. Certain beverages are married to their sports, and I still doubt whether baseball, even the raw, imprecise nature of Triple A, had anything to do with brandy. Brandy, I thought, taking another look at my date as we stood for Steiner's version of "The Star Spangled Banner," which he sprinkled with "Yellow Submarine," brandy is the drink for quoits.

I don't know; I was being a jerk. It wasn't a first. Blame it this time on the eternal unrest that witnessing baseball creates in my breast. There you are ten yards from the field where these guys are *playing*. So close to the fun. I loved baseball. The thing I regretted most was that I hadn't pressed on and played a little minor-league ball. Midgely himself and Snyder, the coach, talked to me that last May, but I was already lost. Nixon was in the White House and baseball just didn't seem relevant activity.

That isn't my greatest regret. I regretted ten other things with equal vigor—well, twelve say. Twelve tops. One in particular. Things that I wanted not to have happened. I wanted Lily back. I wanted to locate the little gumption in my heart that would allow me to step up and go on with my life. I wanted to be fine and strong and quit the law and reach deep and write a big book that some woman on a train would crush to her breast halfway through and sigh. But I could see myself on the table at the autopsy, the doctor turning to the class and looking up from my chest cavity a little puzzled and saying, "I'm glad you're all here for this medical first. He didn't have any. There's no gumption here at all."

I took a big sip of the beer and tried to relax. Brandy's okay in a ballpark, a peccadillo; it was me that was wrong. Lynn rooting around in her big leather purse for her silver flask and smiling so sweetly under the big lights, her face that mysterious thing, varnished with red and amber and the little blue above the eyes, Lynn was just being nice. I thought that: she's just being nice. Then I had the real thought: it's a tough thing to take, this niceness, good luck.

The most prominent feature of any game at Derks is the approximate quality of the pitching. By the third inning we had seen just over a thousand pitches. These kids could throw hard, but it was the catcher who was doing all the work. The wind-up, the pitch, the catcher's violent leap and stab to prevent the ball from imbedding itself in the wire backstop. Just watching him spearing all those wild pitches hurt my knees: up down up down.

I started in, as I always do, explaining the game to Lynn, the fine points. What the different stances indicated about the batters; why the outfielders shifted; how the third baseman is supposed to move to cover the return throw after a move to first. Being a frustrated player, like every other man in America, I wanted to show my skill.

After a few more beers, I settled down. The air cooled, the mountains dimmed, the bright infield rose in the light. I leaned back and just tried to unravel. I listened to Steiner's music, now the theme song from *Exodus,* and I could faintly hear his fans singing, "This land is mine, God gave this land to me . . ." Steiner made me smile. He played what he wanted, when he wanted. In nine innings you could hear lots of Chopin and Liszt, Beethoven, Bartok, and Lennon. He'd play show tunes and commercial jingles. He played lots of rock and roll, and I once heard his version of *An American in Paris* that lasted an inning and a half. He refused to look out and witness the sport that transpired below him. He had met complaints that he didn't get into the spirit of the thing by playing the heady five-note preamble to "Charge!" one night seventy times in a row, until not only was no one calling "Charge!" at the punch line, but the riff had acquired a tangible repulsion in the ears of the management (next door in the press box), and they were quick to have it banished forever. As long as the air was full of organ music, they were happy.

When Steiner did condescend and play "Take Me Out to the Ball Game," he did it in a medley with "In-A-Gadda-Da-Vida" by Iron Butterfly and "Sympathy for the Devil" by the Rolling Stones. The result, obviously, was an incantation for demon worship which his fans loved. And his fans, a group of ten or twelve young kids, done punk, sat below the organ loft with their backs to the game, bobbing their orange heads to Steiner's urgent melodies. This also mollified the management's attitude toward Steiner: the dozen general admission tickets he sold to his groupies alone.

As the game progressed through a series of walks, steals, overthrows, and passed balls, Lynn sipped her brandy and chattered about being out, how fresh it was, how her husband had only taken her to stockholders' meetings, how she didn't really know what to say (that got me a little; shades of actual dating), how being divorced was so different from what she supposed, not really any fun, and how grateful she was that I had agreed to come.

I held it all off. "Come on, this is great. This is baseball."

"Phyllis said you liked baseball."

I didn't lie: "Phyllis is a shrewd cookie."

"She's a good lawyer, but her husband is a shit too." Lynn

tossed back her drink. "You know, Jack, I honestly didn't know anything about marriage when I married my husband. I mean anything." Lynn sipped her brandy. "Clark came back from his mission and he seemed so ready, we just did it. What a deal. He told me later, this is much later, in counseling that he'd spent a lot of time on his mission planning, you know, our sex life. I mean, planning it out. It was awful." She lifted her tiny cup again, tossing back the rest of the drink.

"But," she began again, extending the word to two syllables, "divorce is worse. I don't like being alone. At all. But it's more than that." She looked into my face. "It's just . . . different. Hard." I saw her put her teeth in her lip on the last word, and she closed her eyes. When they opened again, she printed up a smile and showed me the flask. "Are you sure you wouldn't like any?"

"No," I said, kicking back my chair and standing. "I'll get another beer. Be right back."

Under the grandstand, I stood in the beer line and tried to pretend she hadn't shown me her cards. A friend of mine who has had more than his share of difficulty with women not his wife, especially young women not his wife, real young women, called each episode a "scrape." That's a good call. I'd had scrapes too. My second year in law school I took Lisa Krinkel (now Lisa Krink, media person) on a day trip to the mountains. We had a picnic on the Provo River, and I used my skills as a fire-tender and picnic host, along with the accessories of sunshine and red wine, to lull us both into a nifty last-couple-on-earth reverie as we boarded my old car in the brief twilight and headed for home. As always, I hadn't really done anything, except some woody wooing, ten kisses and fingers run along her arm; after all—though I might pretend differently for a day—I was going

with Lily by then. Lisa and I pretended differently all the way
home. I remember thinking: What are you doing, Jack? But
Lisa Krinkel against me in the front seat kept running her fingernails across my chest in a chilling wave down to my belt
buckle, untucking my shirt in the dark and using those fingernails lightly on my stomach, her mouth on my neck, warm, wet,
warm, wet, until my eyes began to rattle. Finally, I pulled into
the wide gravel turnout by the Mountain Meadow Café and told
her either to stop it or deliver.

I wish I could remember exactly how I'd said that. It was
probably something like: "Listen, we'd better not keep that up
because it could lead to something really terrible which we both
would regret forever and ever." But as a man, you can say that in
such an anguished way, twisting in the seat obviously in the ago-
nizing throes of acute arousal, a thing—you want her to
know—so fully consuming and omnivorous that no woman
(even the one who created this monstrous lust) could understand. You writhe, breathing melodramatic plumes of air. You
roll your eyes and adjust your trousers like an animal that would
be better off in every way put out of its misery. And, as I had
hoped, Lisa Krinkel did put me out of my misery with a sudden
startling thrust of her hand and then another minute of those
electric fingernails and some heavy suction on my neck.

Then the strangest thing happened. When she was finished
with my handkerchief, she asked me if we could pray. Well, that
took me by surprise. I was just clasping my belt, but I clasped my
hands humble as a schoolboy while she prayed aloud primarily
to be delivered from evil, which was something I too hoped to be
delivered from, but I sensed the prayer wasn't wholly for me as
she sprinkled it liberally with her boyfriend's name: Tod. She
went on there in the front seat for twenty minutes. I mean if

prayers work, then this one was adequate. That little "Tod" every minute or so kept me alert right to the *amen*. We mounted the roadway and drove on in the dark. It had all changed. Now it seemed real late and it seemed a lot like driving my sister home from her date with Tod. Later I started seeing her on television, where she was a reporter for Channel 3, and it was real strange. Her hair was different, of course, blond, a professional requirement, and her name was different, *Krink*, for some reason, and I could barely remember if I had once had a scrape with this woman (including a couple of four-day nail scratches), if she was a part of my history at all. I mean, watching the news some nights it seemed impossible that I had ever prayed with Lisa Krink.

One of the primary cowardly acts of the late twentieth century is standing beneath the bleachers finishing a new beer before buying another and joining your date. I stood there in the archway, smacking my shoes in a little puddle of water on the cement floor, and tossed back the last of my beer. How lost can you be? The water was from an evaporative cooler mounted up in the locker-room window. It had been dripping steadily onto the floor for a decade. Amazing. I could fix that float seal in ten minutes. I'd done it at our house when Lily and I first moved in. And yet, I stood out of sight wondering how I was going to fix anything else. I bought another beer and went out to join Lynn. Just because you're born into the open world doesn't mean you're not going to have to hide sometimes.

Lynn looked at me with frank relief. I could read it. She thought I had left. I probably should have, but you can't leave a woman alone on this side of town, regardless of how bad the baseball gets.

The quality of Double A baseball is always strained. I could try to explain all the reasons, but there are too many to mention. It is not just a factor of skill or experience, because some of the most dextrous nineteen-year-olds in the universe took the field at the top of every inning along with two or three seasoned vets, guys about to be thirty who had seen action a year or two in the majors. No, it wasn't ability. The problem came most aptly under the title "attitude," and that attitude is best defined as "not giving a shit." It's exacerbated by the fact that not one game in a dozen got a headline and three paragraphs in the *Register* and none of the games were televised. And who—given the times— is going to leave his feet to stop a hot grounder down the line if his efforts are not going to be on TV?

Night fell softly over the lighted ballpark, unlike the dozens of flies that pelted into the outfield. The game bore on and on, both squads using every pitcher in the inventory, and Midgely and the other coach getting as much exercise as anyone by lifting their right and then their left arms to indicate which hurler should file forward next. The pitchers themselves marched quietly from the bull pen to the mound and then twenty pitches later to the dugout and then (we supposed) to the showers. By the time the game ended, after eleven (final score 21 to 16), there were at least four relievers who had showered, shaved, and dressed and were already home in bed.

In an economy measure, the ballpark lights were switched off the minute the last out, a force at second, was completed, and as the afterimage of the field burned out on our eyeballs, we could hear the players swearing as they bumbled around trying to pick their ways into the dugout. Lynn and I fell together and she took my arm so I could lead us stumbling out of the darkened stadium. It was kind of nice right there, a woman on my arm for a purpose, the whole world dark, and through it all the organ music, Steiner Brightenbeeker's mournful version of "Ghost Riders in the Sky." Outside, under the streetlights, the three dozen other souls who had stuck it out all nine innings dispersed, and Lynn and I crossed the street to her car. I looked back at the park. Above the parapet I could see Steiner's cigarette glowing up there in space. I pointed him out to Lynn and started to tell her that I had learned a lot from him, but it didn't come out right. He had always been adamant about his art. He was the one who told me to do something on purpose for art; to go without for it. To skip a date and write a story. That if I did, by two a.m. I'd have fifteen pages and be flying. I couldn't exactly explain it to her, so I just mentioned that he had done the music for the one play I'd ever written a thousand years ago and let it go at that.

At the car we could still hear the song. Steiner would play another hour for his fierce little coterie. The Phantom of the Ballpark.

Lynn and I went to her apartment in Sugarhouse for a nightcap. Now that's a word. Like *cocktail,* which I rarely use, it implies certain protocol. It sounds at first like you are supposed to drink it and get tired, take a few sips and yawn politely and then go to your room. A nightcap. I asked for a beer.

Her apartment was furnished somewhat like the interior of a refrigerator in white plastic and stainless steel, but the sofa was a relatively comfortable amorphous thing that seemed to say, "I'm not really furniture. I'm just waiting here for the future."

The only thing I knew for sure about a nightcap was that there was a moment when the woman said, "Do you mind if I slip into something more comfortable?" I was flipping quickly through the possible replies to such a question when Lynn came back with a pilsner glass full of Beck's for me and a small snifter of brandy for herself. She did not ask if she could slip into something more comfortable; instead she just sat by me in the couch or sofa, that thing, and put her knee up on the seat and her right hand on my shoulder. For a moment then, it was nifty as a picture. I thought: Hey, no problem, a nightcap. This is easy.

"How's your nightcap?" I asked Lynn. We hadn't really talked much in the car or parking it in the basement or riding the elevator to her floor or waiting for her to find her keys and I didn't know how we were doing anymore. Isn't that funny? You see a friend playing the organ in the dark, and you fall asleep at the wheel. I sipped the beer and I had no idea of what to say or do next.

"I love baseball," she breathed at me. She smelled nice, something of brandy and a new little scent, something with a European city in the name of it, and her hand on my shoulder felt good, and I realized, as anyone realizes when he hears a woman tell him a lie when she knows it is a lie and that he is going to know it is a lie and that the rules have been changed or removed and that frankly, he should now do anything he wants to, it's going to be all right. He's not going to get slapped or told, "You fool, what are you doing!" It's a realization that sets the adrenaline on you, your heart, your knees, and I sat there unable to move for a moment as the blood beat my corpuscles open.

When I did move, it was to reach for her, slowly, because that's the best moment, the reach, and I pulled her over toward me to kiss her, but she came with the gesture a little too fully and rolled over on top of me, setting her brandy skillfully on the floor as her mouth closed on mine.

It had been a while for this cowboy, but even so, she didn't quite feel right in my arms. Her body was not the body that I

was used to, that I associated with such pleasures, and her move-
ments too had an alien rhythm which I didn't at first fully appreciate. I was still being dizzied by these special effects when she
started in earnest. It wasn't a moment until we were in a genuine
thumping sofa rodeo, she on top of me, riding for the prize. My
head had been crooked into the corner, stuffed into a spine-
threatening pressure seal, and Lynn was bent (right word here)
on tamping me further into the furniture. She did pause in her
frenzy at one point, arch up, and pull her skirt free, bunching it
at her waist. It was so frankly a practical matter, and her rosy
face shone with such businesslike determination, that it gave me
a new feeling: fear. Supine on that couch device, I suddenly felt
like I was at the dentist. How do these things turn on us? How
does something we seem to want, something we lean toward, instantly grow fangs and offer to bite our heads off?

I remember Midgely at the plate during a college game, going
after what he thought was the fattest fastball he'd ever seen. It
was a slow screwball, and when it broke midway through his
swing and took him in the throat, he looked betrayed. He was
out for a week. He couldn't talk above a whisper until after
graduation. And right now I was midswing with Lynn, and I
could tell something ugly was going to happen.

Meanwhile, with one halfhearted hand on her ass and the
other massaging the sidewall of her breast, I was also thinking:
You don't want to be rude. You don't want to stand, if you
could, and heave her off and run for the door. With her panties
tangled to her knees like that she'd likely take a tumble and put
the corner of something into her brain. There you are visiting
her in the hospital, coma day 183, the room stuffed with bushels
of the flowers you've brought over the last six months, and

you're saying to her sister Phyllis, the most ardent wrongful-death attorney in the history of the world, "Nightcap. We'd had a nightcap."

No, you can't leave. It's a night-cap, and you've got to do your part. You may know you're in trouble, but you've got to stay.

A moment later, Lynn peaked. Her writhing quadrupled suddenly and she went into an extended knee-squeeze seizure, a move I think I had first witnessed on *Big Time Wrestling,* and then she softened with a sigh, and said to me in her new voice, breathy and smiling, a whisper really, "What do you want?"

It's a great question, right? Even when it is misintended as it was here. It was meant here as the perfect overture to sexual compliance, but my answers marched right on by that and lined up. What do I want? *I want my life back. I want to see a chiropractor. I want baseball to be what it used to be.*

But I said, "How about another beer? I should be going soon, but I could use another beer."

When she left the room, shaking her skirt down and then stepping insouciantly out of her underpants, I had a chance to gather my assertiveness. I would tell her I was sorry, but not to call me again. I would tell her I wasn't ready for this mentally or physically. I would tell her simply, Don't be mad, but we're not right for each other *in any way.*

When Lynn reappeared with my beer, I sucked it down quietly and kissing her, took my ambivalent leave. The most assertive thing I said was that I would walk home, that I needed the air. Oh, it was sad out there in the air, walking along the dark streets. Why is it so hard to do things on purpose? I felt I had some principles, why wouldn't they apply? Why couldn't I use one like the right instrument and fix something? Don't answer.

I walked the two miles back to the corner where I used to live, the lost Ghost Mansion. It was as dark as a dark house in a horror film. Was the woman I loved asleep in there? I turned and started down the hill toward my apartment. Oh, I was separated all right, and none of the pieces were big enough to be good for anything. I said Lily's name and made one quiet resolution: no more nightcaps. At all.

DR. SLIME

THIS IS ABOUT the night Betsy told me she was leaving, the night that marked the end of a pretty screwy time all around. Everyone I knew was trying to be an artist, or really was an artist on some scale, and this was in Utah, so you can imagine the scale. Betsy had been almost making a living for several years as a singer, local work for advertising agencies and TV and radio, and my brother Mitchell, who loved her and with whom she lived, was an actor and model for television ads and local theater and whatever movie work came to town. I mean these were people who had consciously said, "I'm going to be an artist no matter what," and that seemed kind of crazy and therefore lovable because it is more interesting than anything nine to five, and I found myself taking care of them from time to time over a three-year period, sponsoring meals and paying their rent two or three times a year, and hanging out with them generally, because I am a regular person, which put me in awe of their refusal to cope with daily duties, and I'll just say it here, rather than let it sneak in later and have you think I'm a vile snake: I came to develop, after the first few months of catching midnight suppers after Mitch's shows and lunches downtown with Betsy after her auditions or after she'd recorded some commercial or other, a condition that anyone in my regular shoes would have developed, I mean not a strange or evil condition, but a profound condition nevertheless, and the condition that I bore night and day was that I was deeply and irrevocably in love with Betsy, my brother's lover, though as you will see it netted me nothing more than a sour and broken heart, broken as regular hearts can be broken, which I probably deserved, no, certainly deserved, and a condition regardless of its magnitude that allowed me to do the noble, the right thing, as you will also see, since I think I acted with grace or at least minor dexterity under such pressure.

I am not an artist. I am a baker for a major supermarket chain and it is work I enjoy more than I should perhaps, but I am dependent on my effort yielding tangible results, and at the end of my shift I go home tired and smelling good. On the day I'm talking about here I came home to my apartment about six a.m. having baked three flights of AUNT DOROTHY's turnovers all night—apple, peach, and raisin—I am AUNT DOROTHY—and found an envelope under the door containing fifteen twenties, the three hundred dollars that Mitch owed me. The note read "THERE IS MORE WHERE THIS CAME FROM. M." Every time he paid me back, this same note was enclosed. It meant that he had found work. His last gig for a smoked-meat ad paid him eight hundred dollars a day for four days, the only work he had in seven months. Mitch was feast or famine.

I put the money in the utility drawer in the kitchen; I would be lending it to him again. I didn't know what it was this time, but Betsy had called a couple of times this week worried, asking about him, what he was doing. He had a big bruise on his neck, and a slug of capsules, unidentifiable multicolored capsules, had begun appearing in the apartment.

"He's an actor," I told her. This is what I used to tell our parents when they would worry. It was a line, I had learned, that was the good news and the bad news at once.

"Yeah, well, I want to know what part beats him up and has him carting drugs."

I wanted to say: So do I, that no-good, erratic beast. Why don't you just drop him and fall into this baker's bed, where you'll be coated in frosting and treated like a goddess. I'll put you on a cake; I'll strew your path with powdered sugar and tender feathers of my piecrusts, for which I am known throughout the Intermountain West.

I said: "Don't worry, Betsy, I'll help you find out."

IT WAS THAT night that she came over to my place on her scooter about seven o'clock and told me she knew something and asked me would I help her, which meant Just Shut Up and Get on the Back. She wore an arresting costume, a red silk shirt printed with little guitars and a pair of bright blue trousers that bloomed at the knees and then fixed tight at the ankle cuff. I scanned her and said, "What decade are we preparing for?"

"Forties," she said, locking up. "Or nineties. You ready? Have you eaten?" I had only been on that red scooter two or three times and found it a terrible and exquisite form of transportation, and the one legitimate opportunity this baker had for putting his hands on the woman who quickened his yeasty heart, in other words, Betsy, my brother's lover, his paramour, his girlfriend, his, his, his.

We took the machine south on State Street. It was exhilarating to be in the rushing air, but the lane changes and a few of the stops made me feel even more tentative than I already did. I held Betsy's waist gingerly, so that at the light on Ninth, he turned and said, "Doug, this is a scooter, hold on for god's sakes. We're friends. Don't start acting like a god damned man." And she clamped my hands onto her sides firmly, my fingers on the top of her hipbones.

That was good, because it made me feel comfortable resting my chin on her shoulder too, as half a joke, and I could feel her smiling as we passed under the streetlights. But the joke was on me, nuzzling a woman of the future, who was I kidding? She smelled fresh, only a little like bread, and though I didn't know it, this was the very apex of my romantic career.

We passed through the rough darkness on Thirty-third South and could see the huge trucks working under lights removing the toxic waste dump where Vitro Processors had been, and then on the rough neon edge of West Valley City, Betsy pulled into Apollo Burger Number Two, a good Greek place. When we stopped I felt the air come up around my face in a little heat. I quickly sidestepped into the bathroom to adjust myself in my underwear; at some point in the close float out here, holding Betsy, my body had begun acting like *a god damned man*.

We ate pastrami burgers and drank cold milk sitting at a sticky picnic table in front of the establishment. It wasn't eight o'clock yet and Betsy assured me we had plenty of time. She knew where we were going because she had asked the driver of the van who had pulled up at their apartment two hours ago. He had come in looking for Mitchell and had told her: Granger High School, eight o'clock. She knew something else, but wasn't telling me.

"He's got to stop taking these stupid nickel-and-dime jobs," she said, as she made a tight ball of her burger wrapper.

"All work has its own dignity," I said—it was one of Mitch's lines.

"Bullshit, it's exploitation. I'm through with it."

"You're not going to sing anymore?"

She stood and threw the paper into a barrel. "I didn't say that."

On the scooter again, I didn't nuzzle. The dinner and the little lesson had taken the spirit out of it for me. I just squinted into the wind and held on. Thirty-fifth South widened into a thick avenue of shopping plazas separated by angry little knots of fast-food joints. Betsy maneuvered us a mile or two and then turned left through a tire outlet parking lot and around a large brick building that I thought was a JC Penney but turned out to be Granger High. We cruised through the parking lot, which was full, and she leaned the scooter against the building. The little marquee above the entrance read: *Welcome Freshmen,* and then below: *Friday, Mack's Mat Matches, 8:00 p.m.*

We stood in a little line of casually dressed Americans at the door and paid four-fifty each for a red ticket which let us into the crowded gymnasium. A vague whomp-whomp we'd been hearing in the hall turned out to be two beefy characters in a raised wrestling ring in the center of the gym slamming each other to the mat.

"Wrestling," I said to Betsy as she led me through the crowd, searching for seats.

"Looks like it."

I followed her, stepping on people's feet all the way across the humid room. There were many family clusters encircled by children standing on the folding chairs and then couples of slumming yuppies, the guy in bright penny loafers and a pastel Lacoste shirt, and sprinkled everywhere small gangs of teenagers in T-shirts waving placards which displayed misspelled death threats toward some of the athletes.

Betsy and I ended up sitting well in the corner of the gym right in the middle of a boiling fan club for the Proud Brothers. Two chubby girls next to me wore Proud Brothers Fan Club T-shirts in canary yellow (the official color) and on the front of each was a drawing of a wrestler's face. The whole club (twelve or so fifteen-year-olds, boys and girls) was hot. They were red in the face and still screaming. Over in the ring, one man would hoist the other aloft and half our neighbors would squeal with vengeful delight, the other half would gasp in horror, and then, after twirling his victim a moment, the wrestler would hurl his opponent to the mat and ka-bang! the whole room would bounce, and the Proud Brothers Fan Club would explode. The noise wanted to tear your hair out. Finally, I noticed that one of the participants had entangled the other's head in the ropes thoroughly and was prancing around the ring in a victory dance. The man in the ropes hung there, his tongue visible thirty rows back, certainly dead. The referee threw up the winner's hands, the bell gonged about twenty times, and the Proud Brothers Fan Club screamed one last time, and the whole gym lapsed into a wonderfully reassuring version of simple crowd noise.

The two girls beside me had fallen into a sisterly embrace, one consoling the other. One girl, her face awash in sweat and tears, peered over her friends' shoulders at me. "Were those the Proud Brothers?" I asked her.

She squeezed her eyes shut in misery and nodded. Her friend turned around to me fully in an odd shoulder-back posture and pulled her T-shirt down tight in what I thought was a gesture meant to display her nubby little breasts, but then she pointed beneath the distorted portrait on the shirtfront to the name below: TOM. Her friend, the bereaved, stood and showed me her breasts too, which were much larger and still heaving from the residual sobs so much that it was difficult to recognize the face on her shirt as human, but I finally read the name underneath: TIM.

"And it was Tim who was just killed?" I asked. She collapsed into her friend's arms again.

Betsy nudged me sharply. "What'd you say to her?" She tapped my arm with her knuckle. "You're going to get arrested. These are children."

By now they had carried the body of one brother away and the other brother had finished his prancing, and the announcer, a little guy in a tux, crawled into the ring with a bullhorn.

"Ladies and gentlemen . . ." he began and before he had finished rolling *gen-tull-mn* out of his mouth, Betsy turned to me and I to her, the same word on our lips: "Mitch!"

We both sat up straight and watched this guy very carefully. It was Mitchell all right, but they had him in a pompadour toupee, a thin mustache, and chrome-frame glasses. What gave him away was his voice and arrow posture and the way he held his chin up like William Tell. He had a good minor strut going around the ring, blasting his phrases in awkward, dramatic little crescendoes at the audience. *"Wee are pleeezd! Tooo pree-zent! A No! Holds! Barred! Un-Ree-Strik-Ted! Marr-eeed Cupples! Tag-Team-Match! Fee-chur-ring Two Dy-nam-ic Du-os! Bobbie and Robbie Hansen! Ver-sus. Mario and Isabella Delsandro!"*

Evidently these were two new dynamic duos, because the crowd was quiet for a moment as people twisted in their seats or stood up to evaluate the contestants. And both couples looked good. Bobbie and Robbie Hansen, I never did find out which was which, were a beefy though not unattractive blond couple who wore matching blue satin wrestling suits. The Delsandros were very handsome people indeed. Mario nodded his beautiful full hairdo at the fans for a moment before dropping his robe and revealing red tights. But it was Isabella who decided the evening. She also had curly black hair and a shiny red suit, but when she waved at the audience, they quieted further. There were some gasps. The girls next to me actually covered their mouths with their hands; I hadn't seen that in real life ever. This was the deal: there was a tuft of hair under each of her arms. It was alien enough for this crowd. Mormon women shave under their arms; it's doctrine. The booing started a second later and when the bell sounded, the fans had made their choice.

When Mitchell ducked out of the ring, Betsy said, "Announcer. That's not bad."

"They've got him up like Sammy Davis, Jr."

"But," she added, "where does an announcer get a black eye?"

I was having trouble taking my eyes from the voluptuous Mrs. Delsandro, who now as the *unclean woman* was getting her ears booed off.

"You're right," I said. "We better stay around, find out what he's up to."

I won't detail the match (or the one after it featuring the snake and the steel cage), but in a sophisticated turn of fate, the Delsandros won. I bounced in my chair the whole forty minutes watching Robbie and Bobbie have at the luckless Mario and Isabella. They were pummeled, tossed, and generously bent.

Then, late in the match, Robbie or Bobbie (Mr. Hansen) was tor-turing Mrs. Delsandro, twisting her arm, gouging her eyes, ren-dering her weaker and weaker. Mr. Delsandro paced and wept in his corner, pulling his hair out, praying to god, and generally making manifest my very feelings for the woman in the ring. Finally Mr. Hansen climbed on the turnstile and leapt on the woozy woman, smashing her to the mat. He was going for the pin. He lay across Mrs. Delsandro this way and that, maneuver-ing cruelly, but every time the referee would slap the mat twice, she'd squirm away. Robbie Hansen or Bobbie Hansen, whatever his name was, was relentless. Mr. Mario Delsandro prayed in his corner of the ring. Evidently his prayers were answered, because about the tenth time the referee slapped the mat twice, Isabella Delsandro bucked and threw Mr. Hansen clear and in a second she was on him. It was such a relief, half the fans cheered.

What she did next sealed the Hansens' fate. She whomped him a good one with a knee drop and then ducked and hoisted him aloft, belly to heaven, in a refreshing spinal stretch. Well, it took the crowd, who thought they were rooting for the home team, less than a second to spot Mr. Hansen as a sick individual. His blue satin shorts bulged precisely with the outline of his skewered erection, and Mrs. Delsandro toured him once around the ring for all to see and then dropped him casually on his head. By now they were urging her, in loud and certain terms, to kill Mr. Hansen. Wrestling is one thing. Transgressing the limits of a family show is entirely another. I heard cries which included the phrases *decapitate, assassinate,* and *put him to sleep.*

She responded by giving him the Norwegian Fish Slap, the Ecuadoran Neck Burn, and the Tap Dance of Death, and then, before tagging her wonderful husband, she stood over the prostrate and slithering Mr. Hansen, her legs apart, her hands on her hips, and she raised her chin triumphantly and laughed. Oh god, it was passion, it was opera, it was giving me the sweats.

When Mario Delsandro leaped into the ring, he swept up his beautiful dark wife and kissed her fully on the mouth. The crowd sang! Mr. Hansen thought he would use the opportunity to crawl away home, but no! Still in the middle of the most significant kiss I've ever witnessed in person, Mr. Delsandro stepped squarely in the middle of Mr. Hansen's back and pressed him flat.

There was never any hope for Mr. Hansen anyway. Among the spectators of his rude tumescence was his wife, Robbie or Bobbie, Mrs. Hansen, and she stood at her corner, her arms crossed as if for the final time, and sneered at him with all her might. Mario Delsandro took his time punishing Mr. Hansen: the German Ear Press, the Thunder Heel Spike, the Prisoner of War, the Ugandan Skull Popper, and the complicated and difficult-to-execute Underbelly Body Mortgage. A few times, early in this parade of torture, Mr. Hansen actually crawled away and reached his corner, where Mr. Delsandro would find him a second later, pleading with his wife to tag him, please tag him, save his life. She refused. At one point while he was begging her for help, she actually turned her back and called to the audience, "Is there a lawyer in the house?" No one responded. The attorneys present realized that to get in between two wrestlers would probably be a mistake.

After taking his revenge plus penalty and interest, Mr. Delsandro tagged the missus, and she danced in and pinned the comatose Mr. Hansen with one finger. The Delsandros kissed and were swept away by the adoring crowd. Mrs. Hansen stalked off. There was a good chance she was already a widow, but the crowd was on its feet and I couldn't see what ever happened to her husband, Mr. Hansen, Robbie or Bobbie.

Mitchell announced the next match, using the same snake oil school of entertaining, which was about right, because, as I said, it involved a snake and a steel cage and five dark men in turbans.

When that carnage was cleared, we found out what we wanted to know. Another announcer, a round man dressed in a black suit carrying what looked like a Bible in his hand, climbed into the ring and introduced the final match of the evening, a grudge match, a match between good and evil if there ever was one, a match important to the very futures of our children, et cetera, et cetera, and here to defend us is David Bright, our brightest star!

Ka-lank! The lights went out. Betsy grabbed my arm. "David Bright?" she said. "Mitch is David Bright?"

"Come to save us all."

An odd noise picked across the top of the room and then exploded into a version of "Onward Christian Soldiers" so loud most people ducked. A razor-edge spotlight flashed on, circling the room once, and then focusing on a crowded corner. In it appeared a phalanx of brown-shirted security guards, all women, marching onward through the teeming crowd. When the entourage reached the ring, we heard the announcer say, "Ladies and gentlemen: David Bright! Our Brightest Star!" And the lights went on and a blond athlete stepped into the ring. He raised his arms once and then took several ministeps to the center of the ring, where he lowered his head in what was supposed to be prayer and bathed in the tumult.

"That's not Mitch." I squinted. "Is it?"

"No," Betsy said. "Look at that guy. There's a lot of praying at these wrestling matches. Is it legal?"

When the crowd slowed a bit and David Bright had gone to his corner and begun a series of simple stretches, the announcer started to speak again. He said, "And his opponent . . ." and couldn't get another word out for all the booing.

I sat down and pulled Betsy to her chair. We looked at each other in that maelstrom of noise. It was a throaty, threatening roar that was certainly made in the jungles when men first began to socialize.

"I think we're about to see Mitch." I told her.

"It sounds as if we're about to see him killed."

"We'll be able to tell by his theme song."

The announcer had continued garbling in the catcalls, and then the lights went out and the spot shot down, circling, and then the sound system blared static and by the first three notes of the song that followed I knew we were in trouble. It was "White Rabbit" by the Jefferson Airplane. The spot fixed on the other corner of the room, and here came a Hell's Angel in a sleeveless black leather jacket, swatting his motorcycle cap at the fans, *get your hands off.* Well, it was a big guy, a large hairy Hell's Angel, a perfect Hell's Angel in my opinion, because it was not my brother Mitchell, and Betsy knew that too, because we exchanged grateful and relieved looks. However, when the Angel reached the ring, he didn't climb up, but bent down and this dirty, skinny person in a red satin robe who had been behind him stepped on the Hell's Angel's back and entered the bright lights of the ring. This guy was Mitchell.

This guy put his face right into all the booing as if it were the sweetest wind on earth. This guy moved slowly, confidently, like Hotspur, which I saw Mitchell play at the Cellar Theater, and he reached into the roomy pockets of his red satin robe and threw handfuls of something at the crowds.

"What's that?" I asked the Proud Brothers fan beside me. The cheerful chubby girl had been my source of information all night.

"Drugs," she said. "He always tries to give drugs to the kids." I could see pills being thrown back into the ring.

Mitchell was laughing.

The announcer closed down his diatribe, which no one could hear, and then yelled, pointing at Mitchell: *"Dr. Slime!"* The booing now tripled, which gave Mitchell such joy he reached down and scooped up a handful of capsules and ate them, grinning.

The bell sounded and Mitchell was still in his robe. David Bright had come forward to wrestle, but Mitchell waved a hand at him, *just a minute*, and poured something on the back of his hand and then snorted it, blowing the residue at the fans. He laughed again, a demented laugh, just like Mephistopheles, which I saw him play at the University Playhouse, coiled his robe, forgot something, unrolled it, removed a syringe, laughed, threw the syringe at the fans, rerolled his robe, and threw it in David Bright's face. David was so surprised by the unfair play that my brother, Dr. Slime, was able to deliver the illegal Elbow Drill to his kidneys. Then while David staggered around on his knees in a daze, removing the robe from his head, Dr. Slime strutted around the ring eating drugs off the mat and waggling his tongue and eyes at those at ringside. From time to time, he'd stop chewing and kick David Bright about the face. The crowd was pissed off. They had rushed the ring and now stood ten deep in the apron. Mitchell could have walked out onto their faces.

He was milking it. I'd seen him do this one other time, in *Macbeth*, running the soliloquies to twice their ordinary length because he sensed an audience with a high tolerance for anguish. Now he knelt and took something from his sock and then snorted it. He leaped in frenzied drug-induced craziness, lest anyone forget he was a maniac, a drug fiend. He whacked the woozy David Bright rapid-fire karatelike blows. He was a whirling dervish.

Then while David Bright still tried to shake off his drubbing and climb to his feet, something happened to Dr. Slime. Something chemical. He kicked David Bright, knocking him down, and raised his arms, his fingers clenched together in (what my female neighbor told me was) his signature attack, the Crashing Bong, and prepared to bring it down on David Bright, ending a promising career. Then Dr. Slime stopped. There he was, mid-ring, his arms up as if holding a fifty-pound hammer, and he froze. Then, of course, he began vibrating, shaking himself out of the pose, his head trembling sickeningly like a tambourine, his hands fluttering full-speed. He began to jerk, drool, and grunt.

His demise couldn't have come at a worse time. David Bright, our brightest star, suddenly came to and stood up. He looked mad. The rest of the match took ten seconds. David Bright, who must have outweighed Mitchell by sixty pounds, picked him up like a rag doll, sorting through his limbs like a burglar, finally grabbing his heels and beginning to spin him around and around like the slingshot that other David used.

Betsy was on my arm with both her hands and when David

Bright let go of Mitchell and Mitchell left the ring and sailed off into the dark, she screamed and jumped on my back to see where he landed. We couldn't see a thing.

The crowd was delighted and David Bright took three or four polite bows, curtsies really, and humbly descended from the light. Betsy was screaming her head off: "You beasts! You fucking animals! I'll kill you all!" Things like that. Things that I would have loved to hear her cry for me.

I was crazy to go find Mitchell or his body or who was responsible for this heinous mayhem and file felony charges, suit, something, but Betsy was broken down, screaming into my shirt by now, and I held her and said *There there*, which is stupid, but I was so glad to have anything to say that I said it over and over.

The auditorium emptied and finally we ended up sitting, worn out, in our seats in the empty corner of the room. My good friend the Proud Brothers fan disappeared and then returned with two yellow T-shirts and gave them to me. "Here," she said. "Glad to meet you. You two are welcome to the club if you can make it next Friday."

I looked down at Betsy, her face wrecked, and I felt my own blood awash with the little chemicals of fear and anger. And love.

"You got the right spirit," the girl said and turned to leave.

We couldn't find Mitchell. We went back through both of the entrances the wrestlers had used, finally running into the school janitor, who simply said, "They don't stay around not one second. They get right in the motor home." He left us alone in the dark corridor.

"Why would he do this?" she said. "Why would he get hooked up with these sleazoid sadists?" She was as beautiful as worried girls get late at night in an empty school.

"I don't know."

"Well, find out!" She said this as an angry order, and then caught herself and smiled. "We've got talk to him, get him out of this."

"Save him," I said.

"What are you saying?" She tilted her head, focusing on me.

"Nothing." Then I decided to go on. "It's just . . . Betsy, I saw him strutting around that ring, playing that crowd."

"And?"

"And: he loved it."

Betsy folded her arms. "He loved having his neck broken."

I wanted to say, Listen, Betsy, it's art. It's all worth it. I had some new information on this subject, having witnessed the Delsandros wrestle, having witnessed their soaring struggle, and having had my heart in their hands, I was a new convert, but what could I say, some guy who is Aunt Dorothy every night in a bakery? I said, "Let's not fight."

She shook her head at me a minute, a phrase in body language that seemed to mean *you pathetic man*. And then we prowled the vacant corridors of Granger High School for a while, from time to time calling, "Mitchell!"

We went into the second-floor girls' room, because we could see the light under the door, and inside she turned to me and said, "Oh hell." It was a four-stall affair, primarily public-school gray with plenty of places to put your sanitary napkins. I could see the back of Betsy's beautiful head in the mirror. There was an old guy standing next to her and when I spoke I realized he was a screwed-up baker out of town for a night with his brother's girlfriend. He looked in serious need of a blood transfusion, exercise, good news.

"Dr. Slime?" I said to the stalls.

"What a night," Betsy said. "It doesn't matter. He's gone."
She leaned against the counter and folded her arms. "He told me
I should tell you my news."

"Good, okay," I said, leaning against the counter too and folding my arms. We stood like that, like two girlfriends in the girls'
room.

"I'm going to L.A. Next week. I have some interviews with
agents and two auditions."

"Auditions?" I said. I am a baker. It is not my job to catch on
quickly. I looked at her face. She was as beautiful as any movie
actress; with her mouth set as it was now and the soft wash of
freckles across her nose and her pale hair up in braids, she
looked twenty. She was smart and she could sing. "You're going
to L.A. You're not coming back here."

"No, I guess I'm not," she said.

"Does Mitchell know?"

"Mitchell knows.

"How hurt is he?"

"That would be a stupid question, wouldn't it, Doug? Don't
you think?"

I took my stupid question and the great load of other stupid
questions forming in my ordinary skull out of the girls' room
and through the dark hallways of Granger High and out into
the great sad night. The parking lot was empty and I stood by
the red scooter as if it were a shrine to the woman I loved, I
ached for, in other words Betsy, who now walked toward me
across the pavement, and who now, I realized, wasn't exactly my
brother's lover anymore, a notion that gave me an odd shiver. I
was as confused as bakers get to be.

"How certain are these things you've got out there?"

"How certain? How certain is my staying here, singing jingles for the next ten years? Come on, Doug: I want to be a singer." She mounted the scooter and waited.

"You are a singer, Betsy. The best. I love your singing. And so, this is your move, right?"

She nodded.

"And it's worth Mitchell?"

She started the machine and the blue exhaust began to roil up into the night. It wasn't a real question and she was right not to answer. Through the raining flux of emotions, worry about Mitchell, love for Betsy, the answer had descended on me like a ton of meringue. I knew the answer. *It was worth it*. It's funny about how the world changes and how art can turn the wheel. I had seen the Delsandros and I had seen my brother, a talented person, an artist, fly through the air to where I knew not, but I knew it was worth it. To be thrown that way in front of two thousand people, well, I'd never done it and I never would, but I know that Mitchell even as he squirmed through the terrific arc of his flight thought it was worth it. That's what art is, perhaps, the look I had seen on his face.

Is this clear? I was annoyed to my baker's bones at these two people and I wanted them to be mine forever. But they were both flying and I was proud of that too. I then climbed on behind my lost love, a woman who sings like an angel and drives a scooter like the devil, that is, Betsy, and I kissed her cheek. Just a little kiss. I wasn't trying anything. "Let us go then," I said, "and see if we can find our close friend Dr. Slime."

DOWN THE
GREEN RIVER

WE WERE FINE. We were holding on to a fine day on the fine Green River in the mountains of Utah five hours from Salt Lake with the sun out and Toby already fishing, when his mother, Glenna, said, "We're sinking." She had been a pain in the ass since dawn. I wanted nothing more than to argue, prove her wrong, but I couldn't because there was real water in the bottom of the raft. You're supposed to leave your troubles behind when you float a river, but given our histories, that was a fat chance.

We were that strange thing: old friends. I'd known Glenna since college; she had been Lily's roommate and there was a time when we were close as close. She had been an ally in my quest for Lily. We'd had a thousand coffees at their kitchen table and she'd counseled and coached me, been a friend. Then after college she had married my pal Warren, which had been her mistake, and I had not married Lily, which had recently (twenty-two days ago) become mine. Warren had not been good to Glenna. His specialty was young women and he used his position as editor of the *Register* to sharpen it. She had grown embittered to say the least, and I wanted now simply to cut that deal—old friends or not—call her a sour unlikable bitch and get on with the day my way; if I had known that she was going to be the photographer for the news story I was writing, I'd have stayed in town.

She had her suitcase—something that has no business even near a raft—balanced on the side tube, and she held her camera case aloft in the other hand. It was dripping. The suitcase made me mad. I was just mad. Glenna had been to Lily's wedding a month (twenty-two days) ago. She had talked to Lily. Now I could see the water over the tops of her shoes in the deep spaces where she stood. It was not common to tear a raft on the gravel, but it happened. I looked downriver for a landing site. The banks were both steep cutaways, but there was a perfect sandbar off to the right side, and I paddled us for it.

After the three of us dragged the raft clear of the water and unloaded the gear, spreading it out to dry, I set Toby at the downstream point with a small Mepps spinner and went back to repair the raft. Glenna was sitting on her suitcase, checking her camera. Her god damned suitcase. Warren had assigned me the story and her the photographs. "Floating the Green"—it would run in Thursday Sports.

I was trying not to think. I had taken the job to get out of town and because I needed the money. Warren said the photographer would pick me up at four a.m., and there in the dark when I saw Glenna's '70 Seville, the same car she'd had at school, my heart clenched. We had all spent a lot of time in that car. And I knew she'd seen Lily. Twenty-two days. If I had been ready, been able to commit; if I had been thirty percent mature; if I had not assumed being more "interesting" than Lily's other dates would keep me first, then I might not have been standing on a sandbar with my teeth in my lip. Did I want to ask Glenna a few questions? Does Lily miss me? Has she said my name? Where should I send her tapes? Yes. Would I? Hey, I had a raft to fix, and as I said, I was trying not to think.

Now sitting on her suitcase on a sandbar, she stretched and reached in her bag for another Merit, which she lit and inhaled. "How'd he talk you into this one?" she said as smoke.

"He mentioned the beauty of nature." I waved up at the sunny gorge, the million facets of the exposed cliffs. "The clear air, the sweet light . . ."

"Bullshit, Jack."

"The money, which I need." I flopped the raft upside down. There were a dozen black patches of various sizes on the bottom, but I could find no new hole. Using my knife, I tested the edges of all the old patches, and, sure enough, one large one was loose. "What about you? You don't need another photo credit."

She pointed at Toby where he fished from the edge of the sand. "I'm here because you know how to do whatever it is we're going to do and you can show it to Toby in some semblance of man-to-boy goodwill and something will have been gained." She flipped the butt into the Green River. "About the rest, I could give a shit. If Warren wants me out of town so he can chase Lolita, so be it."

I bent to my work, scraping at the old patch. I peeled it off and revealed a two-inch L-shaped tear. I wiped the area down and prepared my own new patch with the repair kit while the sun dried the bottom of the raft. I didn't like that phrase *so be it.* There's gloom if not doom in that one.

And sure enough, a moment later Glenna spoke again. "Jack," she said. "Something's happening with the water." Her imprecision almost cheered me, then I looked and saw our sand-bar was shrinking. Toby had reeled in and was walking back, stepping with difficulty in the soft sand.

"Jack," he said. "The water's rising."

I stood still and watched it for a moment. The clear water crawled slowly and surely up the sand. The water was rising.

"My patch isn't dry. Load everything on the raft as it is." I set the cooler and my pack on the upside-down raft and Glenna put her suitcase and Toby placed the sleeping bags and the loose stuff in a heap on the raft. She paused long enough to snap a few photographs of our disaster.

The water inched up, covering our feet, lifting at the raft.

"We're going to get wet now, aren't we?" Glenna said.

"Yes," I said. "Just hold on to the raft and we'll float it down to the gravel spit." I pointed downstream two hundred yards.

"Why is the water rising?" Toby said, laying his pole onto our gear.

"Power for Los Angeles," I told him.

"Some guy's VCR timer just kicked in so he can record *Divorce Court* while he's out playing tennis," Glenna said. "This water is cold!"

Finally enough water crept under the raft to lift it free and we walked it down into the deeper water of the fresh, cold Green River. "Jack," Glenna said, blaming me for hydroelectric power everywhere, "this fucking water is cold!"

"Just hold on," I said to Toby as the water rose toward my chin. "This will be easy."

That is when I saw the next thing, something over my shoulder, and I turned as a small yellow raft drifted swiftly by. There were four women crowded into it. They appeared to be naked.

AN HOUR LATER, we started again. We had clambered out of the river onto the gravel, unloaded the raft, and let the patch air-dry for thirty minutes while Toby and I chose our next series of flies and Glenna, stripped down to her tank top and Levi's, commenced drinking cans of lemon and cherry wine coolers. Then we turned the raft over again, reloaded it, and tenderly made into the river. I immediately pieced Toby's fly rod together, attached the reel, and geared him up with a large Wooly Caddis, the kind of mothy thing that bred thickly on this part of the river. I clipped a bubble five feet from the fly so it would be easier, this early in the day, to handle. Sitting on the side of raft, I began to organize my tackle, and I had to consciously slow myself down. My blood was rich with the free feeling I always get on a river. The sunshine angled down with its first heat of the day on my forearms as I worked, and I realized that my life was a little messy, but for now I was free. It was okay. I was now afloat in a whole different way. It was a feeling a boy has. I smiled with a little rue. Even in a life that is totally waxed, there are still stupid pleasures. It was morning, and I smiled; come on, who hasn't screwed up a life?

Toby had a sharp delivery on his cast, which we worked on for a while as the raft drifted along the smooth sunny river. He was still throwing the line, not punching it into place, but he mastered a kind of effective half-and-half with which he was able to set the fly in the swollen riffles about half the time. It was now late in the morning, but there was enough shade on the water that the fishing could still be good.

I started working the little nymph in the quiet shady pools against the mountain as we'd pass. Once, twice, drift, and back. I saw some sudden shadows and I was too quick on the one rise

I had. Glenna was sitting on her awful suitcase, back against the raft tube, her arms folded, drinking her coolers, quiet as Sunday school behind her oversize dark glasses. From time to time I had to set my rod down and avert the canyon wall or a small boulder or two in the river with the paddle and center us again.

Then later in the morning Glenna took a series of photographs of Toby as he knelt and fly-cast from his end of the raft. She was able, in fact, to film his first fish, a nice twenty-inch rainbow trout which answered the caddis in an odd rocky shallow, coming out of the water to his tail, and Toby, without a scream or a giggle, worked the fish into the current and fifty yards later into our now hot boat. He was a keeper, and Toby said, finally letting his enthusiasm show, "The first one I caught from a raft, ever." I killed the fish on my knee, showing Toby how to tap it smartly behind the cranium, and put him in my creel.

"It's awfully good luck to have the first fish be a keeper," I told him. "Now our nerves are down and we can be generous with the newcomers." Even Glenna seemed pleased watching us, as if her expectations for this sojourn were somehow being met.

I thought about the article I would write. I could have written it without coming, really. I knew the Green by the back. I would talk about the regulations (flies and lures only—no bait); I would talk about the boat launch and the fluctuating river level; I would say take along a patch kit. I would not mention anything that happened next.

The sun had straightened into noon, and the fishing had slowed considerably. I had taken two little trout from pools in the lee of two boulders, handling them with exaggerated care for Toby's information and then returning them to the water.

Then, around the next bend, there was a long slow avenue of river and I found out I had been right about the four rafters. They had been nude. About a half mile down, under a sunny gray shale escarpment, there was a party in session. Eleven or twelve rafts of all sizes had been beached, and fifty or sixty people loitered in the area in a formless nude cocktail party.

"Fish this side of the raft," I said to Toby, adjusting his pole opposite the nudists. Just as I settled him, with a promise of lunkers in that lane, Glenna spotted the other rafters and determined the nature of the activity. She was working down her third wine cooler, a beverage which evoked her less subtle qualities, and she cried out, "Check this out!"

A dozen or so of these noble campers sat bare-assed on a huge fallen log along the river, nursing their beers, taking the sun, watching the river the way people wait for a bus. I heard one call out, "Raft alert! Raft ho!" There was some laughter and a stir of curiosity about our little craft as it drew closer.

I wondered what it was about the wilds that made all these young lawyers feel impelled to take off their clothing. Is it true that as soon as most folks can't see the highway anymore, they immediately disrobe? We came abreast the naked natives in an eerie slow-motion silence. They stopped drawing beer from the keg, quit conversations, stood off the log. Many turned toward us or took half a step toward the river. Glenna was leaning dangerously out of the raft on that side, another wine-cooler casualness (she was just full of wine coolers), and Toby had swiveled fully around from his fishing duties, striking me in the ear with the tip of his rod. I lifted it from his hands.

One bold soul strode down to the edge of the river, waggling himself in the sunshine. He lifted his cup of beer at us and called, "Howdy! What ya doing?" Behind him, still standing against the log, was a slender, dark-haired girl who looked a lot like Lily. She was about as tall and had the posture. Her breasts were pure white, the two whitest things I'd ever seen at noon on a river, a white that hurt the eyes, and her pubic hair glinted red in the bright sunlight. Oh, I don't need to see these things. I need to fish and have my heart start again and be able to breathe without this weight in my chest. I could not physically stop looking at the girl.

"The same thing you are," Glenna answered the young man. "Fishing with worms!" She laughed a full raw laugh back in her throat, leaning so hard on the side of the raft that a quick stream of cold river water sloshed in. As Glenna continued staring the man down and chortling, I thought, This is where it comes from: the devil and the deep blue sea. I am caught, for a moment, between the devil and the deep blue sea. I looked down into the crystal green slip of the river; the stones shimmered and blinked, magnifying themselves in the bent waterlight.

Slowly, we slid past the naked throng. It seemed a blessing that Glenna had not thought to take any photographs. I shifted some of the gear out of the new bilgewater and cast one terrible glance back at the girl and her long bare legs. The arch of her ass along that large smooth log caught my heart like a fishhook. Toby had collapsed like a wet shirt and was sitting on the bottom of the raft, soaking. He bore all the signs of having been electrocuted. I doused his face in a couple handfuls of river water to put out the expression on his face, and sat him up again with his fishing pole and a new lure, a lime-green triple teaser which looked good enough for us to eat. I almost had him convinced that it was still possible to fish in this world when I heard Glenna groan and I felt the raft shift as she stood.

I cursed the pathetic confectioneer who had invented wine coolers and turned to see Glenna reach down and pull her tank top over her head, liberating Romulus and Remus, the mammoth breasts. Shuddered by the shirt, they rippled for a moment and then settled in the fresh air.

"No topless fishing," I said to her. "Don't do that." I handed her the shirt.

She threw it in the river. "I'm not going to fish," she said back to me. Toby had put his pole down again. This river trip had become more dangerous than he'd ever dreamed. I put one hand on his shoulder to restrain him from leaping into the sweet Green River. When I felt him relax, I turned back to Glenna and her titanic nudity. It was still a day. The sun touched off the river in a bright, happy way. We fell out of the long straight stretch into a soft, meandering red canyon. It was still a day.

"Look, Glenna," I said. She had opened another wine cooler. "Look. We're going to fish. This is a raft trip and we're going to fish. It would help everything if you would take your drink and turn around and face forward. Either way, you're going to get a wicked sunburn." I moved the three plastic-covered sleeping bags in such a way as to make her a backrest. She looked at me defiantly, and then she turned her back and settled in.

It was still a day. I took the bubble off Toby's line and showed him how to troll the triple teaser. "There are fish here," I told him. "Let's go to work." I tied an oversize Royal Coachman on my line and began casting my side of the river, humming—for some reason—the Vaughn Monroe version of the ominous ballad "Ghost Riders in the Sky." I knew the words, even the yippie-ai-ais.

WE PASSED LITTLE HOLE at three o'clock and I knew things would get better. Ninety-nine percent of the rafters climb out at Little Hole and we could see two dozen big GMC pickups and campers waiting in the parking lot. We'd already passed a flotilla of Scout rafts all tethered together in a large eddy taking fly-casting lessons. It was a relief to see that they didn't have enough gear to spend the night on the river.

It had been an odd scene, all those little men in their decorated uniforms, nodding seriously into the face of their leader, a guy about my age who was standing on a rock with his flyrod, explaining the backcast. It was his face as it widened in surprise that signaled the troop to turn and observe what would be for many of them the largest breasts they would ever witness in person no matter how long they lived. Glenna had smiled easily at all of them and waved sweetly at their leader. I said nothing, but put my pole down and paddled hard downstream, just in case Glenna had really got to the guy and brought out the incipient vigilante all Scout leaders have. I didn't want to be entangled in some midstream citizen's arrest.

Anyway, it was a relief to pass Little Hole and know that we would see no more human beings until tomorrow noon when we'd land at Brown's Park and the end of trail, so to speak.

By this time, Glenna was relaxed. She'd slowed her drinking (and her speech and about everything else) and seemed to be in a kind of happy low-grade coma, bare breasted in the prow of our ship like some laid-back figurehead. Toby had been doing well with the triple teaser, taking three small trout, which we'd released. He handled the fish skillfully and made sure they returned to the river in good shape. I had had nothing on the Coachman, but it was not the fly's fault. I had been casting in time with "Ghost Riders in the Sky":

> Then cowboy change your ways today, (cast)
> Or with us you will ride, (cast)

and a fish would have lucky to even catch a glimpse of its fur.

A-trying to catch the Devil's herd (cast)
Across these endless skies. (cast)

So there had been a little pressure, but now the long green shadows dragged themselves languorously across the clear water. It was late afternoon. We were past Little Hole. It was still a day. We dropped around two bends and were suddenly in the real wilderness, I could feel it, and I felt that little charge that the real places give me.

I had been here before, of course, many times with Lily. In the old days I thickened my favorite books in the bottom of rafts. Lily and I would leave the city Friday night, spend two days fishing scrupulously down the Green River, and drive back five hours from Brown's Park in the dark, arriving back in town in time for class with a giveaway suntan and the taste of adrenaline in my mouth. My books, *The Romantic Poets, The Victorian Poets, Eons of Literature,* were all swollen and twisted, their pages still wet as I sat in class, some of them singed where I had tried to dry them by the fire. Those trips with Lily were excruciatingly one-of-a-kind ventures—the world, planet and desire, fused and we had our way with it. I remember it all. I remember great poetry roasting cheerily by the fire in some lone canyon while Lily and I lay under the stars. Those beautiful books, I still have them.

MY LINE TRIPPED once hard and then I felt another sharp tug as my Royal Coachman snapped away in the mouth of what could only be a keeper. I set the hook and measured the tension. The trout ran. I gave him line evenly as the pressure rose, and he broke the surface, sixty yards behind us in the dark swelling river.

"Whoa!" Toby said.

"Watch your line, son," I told him. "It's the perfect time of night."

But even as I worked the trout stubbornly forward in the river, I was thinking about Lily. I'd never grown up and now fishing wasn't even the same.

THAT FISH WAS a keeper, a twenty-inch brown, and so were the two Toby took around the next bend as we passed under a monstrous spruce that leaned over the water. Four hills later we drifted into the narrows of Red Canyon. It was the deep middle of the everlasting summer twilight, and I cranked us over to the bank, booting the old wooden oars hard on the shallow rocky bottom. We came ashore halfway down the gorge so we could make camp. The rocky cliffs had gone coral in the purple sky and the river glowed green behind us as we unloaded the raft.

Glenna finally grabbed another T-shirt and struggled into it, something about being on land, I suppose, and said, "Oh, I gotta pee!" stepping stiffly up the sage-grown shore.

By the time she returned, the darkness had thickened, and Toby and I had a small driftwood fire going and were clearing an area for the tents. Glenna hugged herself against the fresh air coming along the river. She was a little pie-faced, but opened another wine cooler anyway. I fetched a flannel shirt from my kit and gave it to Toby, and then I settled down to the business of frying those fish. Since we were having cocktails, Glenna already reclining before the fire, I decided to take the extra time and make trout chowder.

Here's how: I retrieved my satchel of goodies, including a half pint of Old Kilroy, which is a good thing to sip if you're going to be cooking trout over an open fire while the night cools right down. In there too was a small tin of lard. You use about a table-spoon of lard for each trout, melting it in the frying pan and placing the trout in when the pan is warm, not hot. If the pan is too hot the fish will curl up and make it tricky cooking. If you don't have lard or butter, it's okay. Usually you don't. Without it you have to cook the trout slower, preventing it from sticking and burning in the pan by sprinkling in water and continuously prodding the fish around. Cut off the heads so the fish will fit into the pan. Then slice both onions you brought and let them start to cook around the fish. At the same time, fill your largest pot with water and put it on to boil. In Utah now you have to boil almost all your water. There is a good chance that someone has murdered his neighbor on instructions from god and thrown him in the creek just upstream from where you're mak-ing soup. Regardless, with a river that goes up and down eight inches twice a day, you have a lot of general cooties streaming right along. This is a good time to reach into the pack and peel open a couple cans of sardines in mustard sauce as appetizers, passing them around in the tin along with your Forest Master pocketknife, so the diners can spear a few and pass it on.

Okay, by the time your water boils, you will have fried the trout. When they've cooled, it will be easy to bone them, starting at the tail and lifting the skeleton from each. This will leave you with a platter of trout pieces. Add a package of leek soup mix (or vegetable soup mix) to the boiling water and then a package of tomato soup mix (or mushroom soup mix) and then the fried onion and some garlic powder. Then slip the trout morsels into the hot soup and cook the whole thing for another twenty min-utes while you drink whiskey and mind the fire. You want it to thicken up. Got any condensed milk? Add some powdered milk at least. Stir it occasionally. Pepper is good to add about now, too. When it reaches the consistency of gumbo, break out the bowls. Serve it with hunks of bread and maybe a slab of sharp cheddar cheese thrown across the top. It's a good dinner, easier to eat in the dark than a fried trout, and it stays hot longer and contains the foods that real raftsmen need. Bitter women who have been half naked all day drinking alcoholic beverages will eat trout chowder with gusto, not talking, just sopping it up, cheese, bread, and all. Be prepared to serve seconds.

AFTER HER SECOND bowl, her mouth still full of bread, Glenna said, "So, quite a day, eh, Jack?"

"Five good fish," I said, nodding at Toby. "Quite a day."

"No, I mean . . ."

"I know what you mean." I moved the pot of chowder off the hot ring of rocks around the fire and set it back on the sand, securing the lid. "We rescued a day from the jaws of the nudists."

The cooking had calmed me down, and I didn't want to get started with Glenna, especially since she was full of fructose and wine. Cooking, they say, uses a different part of your brain and I know which part, the good part, the part that's not wired all screwy with your twelve sorry versions of your personal history and the four jillion second guesses, backward glances, forehead-slapping embarrassments. The cooking part is clean as a cutting board and fitted accurately with close measurements and easy-to-follow instructions, which, you always know, are going to result in something edible and nourishing, over which you could make real conversation with someone, maybe someone you've known since college.

I ran the crust of my bread around the rim of my bowl and ate the last bite of chowder. It was good to be out of the raft, sitting on the ground by the fire, but I could feel there was going to be something before everybody hit the hay.

"Did you have fun, honey?" Glenna said to Toby. "Are you glad you came?"

"Yeah."

"Do you like old Jack here?"

"Aw, he's okay," I said and smiled at Toby.

"I've known Jack a long time."

"I know," Toby said.

"When did we meet, Jack?"

I broke some of the driftwood smaller in my hands and fed the fire back up. Toby had already filled the other kettle with water and I balanced it over the flames on three rocks.

"You want some coffee?" I said. I did not want to get started on the old world. We had met in the lobby of Wasatch Dorm my junior year. Glenna had come up to take my picture for the *Chronicle*. It was the Christmas of the White Album and Warren had decided I should run for class president. That afternoon she introduced me to her roommate, Lily Westerman.

"I don't think so," she said, showing me her bottle of Cabernet Lemon-Lime.

"Get your cup, Toby," I said. When I heard the boiling water cracking against the side of the kettle, I poured him a cup of hot chocolate. I fixed myself a cup of instant coffee and poured in a good lick of whiskey. Toby was standing to one side, a bright silhouette in the firelight.

"I think I'll go to bed," he said. "You guys are going to talk ancient history for a while. Dad was a big man on campus. This was during the war and he ran the paper, and Mom was the head photographer. You were all students, sort of, and Jack was going with Lily, who was Mom's roommate, and their house was like a club in the days when things mattered." He sipped his chocolate and toasted us. He knew how smart he was. "This was years ago."

"He's older than I am."

"Oh Jack," Glenna said, suddenly looking at me with eyes as cool and sober as the night. "Everybody's older than you are. That's always been your thing. It's kind of cute—about half." She must have seen me listening too hard, because she immediately waved her hand in front of her face and said, "Jack, ignore me. I'm drunk. That's what I do now: the drunk housewife."

"I don't believe her," I told Toby.

"I don't either," he said.

"Are you mad at your mother for embarrassing you today?" Glenna said. She was slumped against a rock opposite me. Her voice was now husky from too much sun, too much wine, too much lemon-lime.

"Mom," Toby said. "I'm tired. It was a pretty wild day. Good night." And he stepped down through the sage to his tent.

Halfway in the dark, he turned. "But Mom, you know what you said to that guy today, the naked guy?"

"Yeah?"

"It wasn't right. We weren't fishing with worms. The Green River is artificial flies and lures only."

"Okay, honey."

"But it was pretty funny, given the situation." He nodded once at us. "Good night." Toby disappeared in the dark.

"He's a good kid," I said.

She nodded the way people nod when their eyes are full and to speak would be to cry.

"It's okay," I said. "It was a good day." I looked at her

slumped on her suitcase, her hideous and beautiful suitcase, which seemed now simply something else trying to break my heart.

"Oh, Jack, I'm sorry. I'm so surprised by what I do, what anybody does. I guess I'm surprised any of it gets to me. If we'd just met, this would be a fun trip. If we were strangers. We're two people who know too much."

It was the worst kind of talk I'd ever heard around a campfire, and I wanted it to go away. "You're all right," I said. "You've got Toby." That, evidently, of course, was exactly the wrong thing to say and I sensed this from what I could hear in Glenna's breath. She was going to cry. The whole night seemed wrong.

I could hear a high wind in the junipers, but it was quiet in our camp. The campfire fluttered and sucked, settling down. I stared into the pink coals and watched them pulse white. I could see the bright edge of light on the cliff tip that meant in an hour the moon would break over the canyon. The other noise that came along sure as sure was the soft broken sucking of Glenna crying. She had her hand over her face in a gesture of real grief. I watched her for a moment, holding myself still. I was going to cry too, but I was going to try to wait for the moon. Finally, I went around the dying fire and sat by her.

"Hey, Glenna. Glenna," I whispered. "Did you bring any sunburn stuff?"

She shook her head no.

"Here," I said, handing her my tube of aloe. "Use this tonight. Okay? Use plenty. You surely scorched yourself." I could feel the heat from her sunburn as I sat by her.

"He's a good kid," she said.

"He's a great kid."

She shuddered and drew up in a series of short serious sobs. When that wave passed, I said, "What's the matter?" We were both speaking quietly.

She shook her head again, this time as if shaking something off. She said, "You're bright and young and you get married and you kind of always have money and then, bang-o, a thousand people later you're sunburned and eating fish in the big woods with an old friend and only the smallest part of it seems like the center of your life anymore. What's that about?"

I was beyond speaking now, lost in a widening orbit miles from our little fire. I knew she was going to go on. "There is a message, you know. From Lily. We saw her at the wedding." It had taken her all day but she had finally said Lily's name. "It's terrible, of course. We were eating cake and she came over to our table and said to tell Jack hello. So, *hello*."

Now I had to hold her. Someone offers you that kind of last hello and whether you're camped by the river or not, you'll probably hug her, feeling her pulsing sunburn, and sit there thinking it all over for a little while. I had forever turned some corner in my life this month (twenty-two days), but I hadn't known it until Glenna said hello. Like it or not I was through being a boy.

So be it.

We sat there quietly and soon—over the steady low flash of the river—I could hear Toby, down in his tent, humming. It was something familiar, a sad ballad involving the devil's cattle and a long ride.

OXYGEN

IN 1967, THE year before the year that finally cracked the twentieth century once and for all, I had as my summer job delivering medical oxygen in Phoenix, Arizona. I was a sophomore at the University of Montana in Missoula, but my parents lived in Phoenix, and my father, as a welding engineer, used his contacts to get me a job at Ayr Oxygen Company. I started there doing what I called dumbbell maintenance, the kind of makework assigned to college kids. I cleared debris from the back lot, mainly crushed packing crates that had been discarded. That took a week, and on the last day, as I was raking, I put a nail through the bottom of my foot and had to go for a tetanus shot. Next, I whitewashed the front of the supply store and did such a good job that I began a month of painting my way around the ten-acre plant.

These were good days for me. I was nineteen years old and this was the hardest work I had ever done. The days were stunning, starting hot and growing insistently hotter. My first week two of the days had been 116. The heat was a pure physical thing, magnified by the steel and pavement of the plant, and in that first week, I learned what not to touch, where not to stand, and I found the powerhouse heat simply bracing. I lost some of the winter dormitory fat and could feel myself browning and getting into shape. It felt good to pull on my Levi's and work-shoes every morning (I'd tossed my tennies after the nail incident), and not to have any papers due for any class.

Of course, during this time I was living at home, that is arriving home from work sometime after six and then leaving for work sometime before seven the next morning. My parents and I had little use for each other. They were in their mid-forties then, an age I've since found out that can be oddly taxing, and besides they were in the middle of a huge career decision which would make their fortune and allow them to live the way they live now. I was nineteen, as I said, which in this country is not a real age at all, and effectively disqualifies a person for one year from meaningful relationship with any other human being.

I was having a hard ride through the one relationship I had begun during the school year. Her name was Linda Enright, a classmate, and we had made the mistake of sleeping together that spring, just once, but it wrecked absolutely everything. We were dreamy beforehand, the kind of couple who walked real close, bumping foreheads. We read each other's papers. I'm not making this up: we read poetry on the library lawn under a tree. I had met her in a huge section of Western Civilization taught by a young firebrand named Whisner, whose credo was "Western civilization is what you personally are doing." He'd defined it that way the first day of class and some wit had called out, "Then Western Civ is watching television." But Linda and I had taken it seriously, the way we took all things I guess, and we joined the Democratic Student Alliance and worked on a grape boycott, though it didn't seem that there were that many grapes to begin with in Montana that chilly spring.

And then one night in her dorm room we went ahead with it, squirming out of our clothes on her hard bed, and we did something for about a minute that changed everything. After that we weren't even the same people. She wasn't she and I wasn't I; we were two young citizens in the wrong country. I see now that a great deal of it was double-and triple-think, that is I thought she thought it was my fault and I thought that she might be right with that thought and I should be sorry and that I was sure she didn't know how sorry I was already, regret like a big burning house on the hill of my conscience, or something like that, and besides all I could think through all my sorrow and compunction was that I wanted it to happen again, soon. It was confusing. All I could remember from the incident itself was Linda stopping once and undoing my belt and saying, "Here, I'll get it."

The coolness of that practical phrase repeated in my mind after I'd said goodbye to Linda and she'd gone off to Boulder, where her summer job was working in her parents' cookie shop. I called her every Sunday from a pay phone at an Exxon Station on Indian School Road, and we'd fight and if you asked me what we fought about I couldn't tell you. We both felt misunderstood. I knew I was misunderstood, because I didn't understand myself. It was a glass booth, the standard phone booth, and at five in the afternoon on a late-June Sunday the sun torched the little space into a furnace. The steel tray was too hot to fry eggs on, you'd have ruined them. It gave me little burns along my forearms. I'd slump outside the door as far as the steel cord allowed, my skin running to chills in the heat, and we'd argue until the operator came on and then I'd dump eight dollars of quarters into the blistering mechanism and go home.

The radio that summer played a strange mix, "Little Red Riding Hood," by Sam the Sham and the Pharaohs, over and over, along with songs by the Animals, even "Sky Pilot." This was not great music and I knew it at the time, but it all set me on edge. After work I'd shower and throw myself on the couch in my parents' dark and cool living room and read and sleep and watch the late movies, making a list of the titles eventually in the one notebook I was keeping.

About the third week of June, I burned myself. I'd graduated to the paint sprayer and was coating the caustic towers in the oxygen plant. These were two narrow, four-story tanks that stood beside the metal building where the oxygen was bottled. The towers were full of a viscous caustic material that air was forced through to remove nitrogen and other elements until the gas that emerged was 99 percent oxygen. I was forty feet up an extension ladder reaching right and left to spray the tops of the tanks. Beneath me was the pump station that ran the operation, a nasty tangle of motors, belts, and valving. The mistake I made was to spray where the ladder arms met the curved surface of the tank, and as I reached out then to hit the last and farthest spot, I felt the ladder slide in the new paint. Involuntarily I threw my arms straight out in a terrific hug against the super-heated steel. Oddly I didn't feel the burn at first nor did I drop the spray gun. I looked down at what seemed now to be the wicked machinery of my death. It certainly would have killed me to fall. After a moment, and that's the right span here, a moment, seconds or a minute, long enough to stablilize my heartbeat and sear my cheekbone and the inside of both elbows, I slid one foot down one rung and began to descend.

All the burns were the shapes of little footballs, the one on my face a three-inch oval below my left eye, but after an hour with the doctor that afternoon, I didn't miss a day of work. They've all healed extraordinarily well, though they darken first if I'm not careful with the sun. That summer I was proud of them, the way I was proud not to have dropped the spray gun, and proud of my growing strength, of the way I'd broken in my workshoes, and proud in a strange way of my loneliness.

Where does loneliness live in the body? How many kinds of loneliness are there? Mine was the loneliness of the college student in a summer job at once very far from and very close to the thing he will become. I thought my parents were hopelessly bourgeois, my girlfriend a separate race, my body a thing of wonder and terror, and as I went through the days, my loneliness built. Where? In my heart? It didn't feel like my heart. The loneliness in me was a dryness in the back of my mouth that could not be slaked.

And what about lust, that thing that seemed to have defeated me that spring, undermined my sense of the good boy I'd been, and rinsed the sweetness from my relationship with Linda? Lust felt related to the loneliness, part of the dry, bittersweet taste in the lava-hot air. It went with me like an aura as I strode with my three burns across the paved yard of Ayr Oxygen Company, and I felt it as a certain tension in the tendons in my legs, behind the knees, a tight, wired feeling that I knew to be sexual.

THE LOADING DOCK at Ayr Oxygen was a huge rotting concrete slab under an old corrugated-metal roof. Mr. Mac Bonner ran the dock with two Hispanic guys that I got to know pretty well, Victor and Jesse, and they kept the place clean and well organized in a kind of military way. Industrial and medical trucks were always delivering full or empty cylinders or taking them away, and the tanks had to be lodged in neat squadrons which would not be in the way. Victor, who was the older man, taught me how to roll two cylinders at once while I walked, turning my hands on the caps and kick-turning the bottom of the rear one. As soon as I could do that, briskly moving two at a time, I was accepted there and fell into a week of work with them, loading and unloading trucks. They were quiet men who knew the code and didn't have to speak or call instructions when a truck backed in. I followed their lead.

The fascinating thing about Victor and Jesse was their lunches. I had been eating my lunch at a little patio behind the main building, alone, not talking to the five or six other employees who sat in groups at the other metal tables. I was the college kid and they were afraid of me because they knew my dad knew one of the bosses. It seemed there had been some trouble in previous summers, and so I just ate my tuna sandwiches and drank my iced tea while the sweat dried on my forehead and I pulled my wet T-shirt away from my shoulders. After I burned my face, people were friendlier, but then I was transferred up to the dock.

There were dozens of little alcoves amid the gas cylinders standing on the platform, and that is where I ate my lunches now. Victor and Jesse had milk crates and they found one for me and we'd sit out of sight up there from eleven-thirty to noon and eat. There was a certain uneasiness at first, as if they weren't sure if I should be joining them, but then Victor saw it was essentially a necessity. I wasn't going to get my lunch out of the old fridge on the dock and walk across the yard to eat with the supply people. On the dock was where I learned the meaning of *whitebread,* the way it's used now. I'd open my little bag, two tuna sandwiches and a baggie of chips, and then I'd watch the two men open their huge sacks of burritos and tacos and other items I didn't know the names of and which I've never seen since. I mean these were huge lunches that their wives had prepared, everything wrapped in white paper. No baggies. Jesse and I traded a little bit; he liked my mother's tuna. And I loved the big burritos. I was hungry and thirsty all the time and the hefty food seemed to make me well for a while. The burritos were packed with roast beef and onions and a fiery salsa rich with cilantro. During these lunches Victor would talk a little, telling me where to keep my gloves so that the drivers didn't pick them up, and where not to sit even on break.

"There was a kid here last year," he said. "Used to take his breaks right over there." He shook his head. "Right in front of the boss's window." It was cool and private sitting behind the walls of cylinders.

"He didn't stay," Jesse said. "The boss don't know you're on break."

"Come back in here," Victor said. "Or don't sit down." He smiled at me. I looked at Jesse and he shrugged and smiled too. They hadn't told the other kid where not to sit. Jesse handed me a burrito rolled in white paper. I was on the inside now; they'd taken me in.

That afternoon there was a big Linde Oxygen semi backed against the dock and we were rolling the hot cylinders off when I heard a crash. Jesse yelled from back in the dock and I saw his arms flash and Victor, who was in front of me, laid the two tanks he was rolling on the deck of the truck and jumped off the side and ran into the open yard. I saw the first rows of tanks start to tumble wildly, a chain reaction, a murderous thundering domino chase. As the cylinders fell off the dock, they cartwheeled into the air crazily, heavily tearing clods from the cement dock ledge and thudding into the tarry asphalt. A dozen plummeted onto somebody's Dodge rental car parked too close to the action. It was crushed. The noise was ponderous, painful, and the session continued through a minute until there was only one lone bank of brown nitrogen cylinders standing like a little jury on the back corner of the loading dock. The space looked strange that empty.

The yard was full of people standing back in a crescent. Then I saw Victor step forward and walk toward where I stood on the back of the semi. I still had my hands on the tanks.

He looked what? Scared, disgusted, and a little amused. "Mi amigo," he said, climbing back on the truck. "When they go like that, run away." He pointed back to where all of the employees of Ayr Oxygen Company were watching us. "Away, get it?"

"Yes, sir," I told him. "I do."

"Now you can park those," he said, tapping the cylinders in my hand. "And we'll go pick up all these others."

It took the rest of the day and still stands as the afternoon during which I lifted more weight than any other in this life. It felt a little funny setting the hundreds of cylinders back on the old pitted concrete. "They should repour this," I said to Victor as we were finishing.

"They should," he said. "But if accidents are going to follow you, a new floor won't help." I wondered if he meant that I'd been responsible for the catastrophe. I had rolled and parked a dozen tanks when things blew, but I never considered that it might have been my fault, one cockeyed tank left wobbling.

"I'm through with accidents," I told him. "Don't worry. This is my third. I'm finished."

The next day I was drafted to drive one of the two medical

oxygen trucks. One of the drivers had quit and our foreman, Mac Bonner, came out onto the dock in the morning and told me to see Nadine, who ran Medical, in her little office building out front. She was a large woman who had one speed: gruff. I was instructed in a three-minute speech to go get my commercial driver's license that afternoon and then stop by the uniform shop on Bethany Home Road and get two sets of the brown trousers and short-sleeved yellow shirts worn by the delivery people. On my way out I went by and got my lunch and saw Victor. "They want me to drive the truck. Dennis quit, I guess." This was new to me and I was still working it over in my mind; I mean, it seemed like good news.

"Dennis wouldn't last," Victor said. "We'll have the Ford loaded for you by nine."

The yellow shirt had a name oval over the heart pocket: David. And the brown pants had a crease that will outlast us all. It felt funny going to work in those clothes and when I came up to the loading dock after picking up the truck keys and my delivery list, Jesse and Victor came out of the forest of cylinders grinning. Jesse saluted. I was embarrassed and uneasy. "One of you guys take the truck," I said.

"No way, David." Victor stepped up and pulled my collar straight. "You look too good. Besides, this job needs a white guy." I looked helplessly at Jesse.

"Better you than me," he said. They had the truck loaded: two groups of ten medical blue cylinders chain-hitched into the front of the bed. They'd used the special cardboard sleeves we had for medical gas on all the tanks; these kept them from getting too beat up. These tanks were going to be in people's bedrooms. Inside each was the same oxygen as in the dinged-up green cylinders that the welding shops used.

I climbed in the truck and started it up. Victor had already told me about allowing a little more stopping time because of the load. "Here he comes, ladies," Jesse called. I could see his hand raised in the rearview mirror as I pulled onto McDowell and headed for Sun City.

At that time, Sun City was set alone in the desert, a weird theme park for retired white people, and from the beginning it gave me an eerie feeling. The streets were like toy streets, narrow and clean, running in huge circles. No cars, no garage doors open, and, of course, in the heat, no pedestrians. As I made my rounds, wheeling the hot blue tanks up the driveways and through the carpeted houses to the bedroom, uncoupling the old tank, connecting the new one, I felt peculiar. In the houses I was met by the wife or the husband and was escorted along the way. Whoever was sick was in the other room. It was all very proper. These people had come here from the midwest and the east. They had been doctors and professors and lawyers and wanted to live among their own kind. No one under twenty could reside in Sun City. When I'd made my six calls, I fled that town, heading east on old Bell Road, which in those days was miles and miles of desert and orchards, not two traffic lights all the way to Scottsdale Road.

Mr. Rensdale was the first of my customers I ever saw in bed. He lived in one of the many blocks of townhouses they were building in Scottsdale. These were compact units with two stories and a pool in the small private yard. All of Scottsdale shuddered under bulldozers that year; it was dust and construction delays, as the little town began to see the future. I rang the bell and was met by a young woman in a long silk shirt who saw me and said, "Oh, yeah. Come on in. Where's Dennis?"

I had the hot blue cylinder on the single dolly and pulled it up the step and into the dark, cool space. I had my pocket rag and wiped the wheels as soon as she shut the door. I could see her knees and they seemed to glow in the near dark. "I'm taking his route for a while," I said, standing up. I couldn't see her face, but she had a hand on one hip.

"Right," she said. "He got fired."

"I don't know about that," I said. I pointed down the hall. "Is it this way?"

"No, upstairs, first door on your right. He's awake, David." She said my name just the way you read names off shirts. Then she put her hand on my sleeve and said, "Who hit you?" My burn was still raw across my cheekbone.

"I got burned."

"Cute," she said. "They're going to love that back at . . . where?"

"University of Montana," I said.

"University of what?" she said. "There's a university there?" She cocked her head at me. I couldn't tell what she was wearing under that shirt. She smiled. "I'm kidding. I'm a snob, but I'm kidding. What year are you?"

"I'll be a junior," I said.

"I'm a senior at Penn," she said. I nodded, my mind whipping around for something clever. I didn't even know where Penn was.

"Great," I said. I started up the stairs.

"Yeah," she said, turning. "Great."

I drew the dolly up the carpeted stair carefully, my first second story, and entered the bedroom. It was dim in there, but I could see the other cylinder beside the bed and a man in the bed, awake. He was wearing pajamas, and immediately upon seeing me, he said, "Good. Open the blinds, will you?"

"Sure thing," I said, and I went around the bed and turned the miniblind wand. The Arizona day fell into the room. The young woman I'd spoken to walked out to the pool beneath me. She took her shirt off and hung it on one of the chairs. Her breasts were white in the sunlight. She set out her magazine and drink by one of the lounges and lay facedown in a shiny green bikini bottom. I only looked down for a second or less, but I could feel the image in my body.

While I was disconnecting the regulator from the old tank and setting up the new one, Mr. Rensdale introduced himself. He was a thin, handsome man with dark hair and mustache and he looked like about three or four of the actors I was seeing those nights in late movies after my parents went to bed. He wore an aspirator with the two small nostril tubes, which he removed while I changed tanks. I liked him immediately. "Yeah," he went on, "it's good you're going back to college. Though there's a future, believe me, in this stuff." He knocked the oxygen tank with his knuckle.

"What field are you in?" I asked him. He seemed so absolutely worldly there, his wry eyes and his East Coast accent, and he seemed old the way people did then, but I realize now he wasn't fifty.

"I, lad, am the owner of Rensdale Foundations, which my father founded," his whisper was rich with humor, "and which supplies me with more money than my fine daughters will ever be able to spend." He turned his head toward me. "We make ladies' undergarments, lots of them."

The dolly was loaded and I was ready to go. "Do you enjoy it? Has it been a good thing to do?"

"Oh, for chrissakes," he wheezed a kind of laugh, "give me a week on that, will you? I didn't know this was going to be an interview. Come after four and it's worth a martini to you, kid, and we'll do some career counseling."

"You all set?" I said as I moved to the door.

"Set," he whispered now, rearranging his aspirator. "Oh absolutely. Go get them, champ." He gave me a thin smile and I left. Letting myself out of the dark downstairs, I did an odd thing. I stood still in the house. I had talked to her right here. I saw her breasts again in the bright light. No one knew where I was.

Of course, Elizabeth Rensdale, seeing her at the pool that way, so casually naked, made me think of Linda and the fact that I had no idea of what was going on. I couldn't remember her body, though, that summer, I gave it some thought. It was worse not being a virgin, because I should have then had some information to fuel my struggles with loneliness. I had none, except Linda's face and her voice, *"Here, let me get it."*

From the truck I called Nadine, telling her I was finished with Scottsdale and was heading—on schedule—to Mesa. "Did you pick up Mr. Rensdale's walker? Over."

"No, ma'am. Over." We had to say "Over."

"Why not? You were supposed to. Over."

The heat in the early afternoon as I dropped through the river bottom and headed out to Mesa was gigantic, an enormous, unrelenting thing, and I took a kind of perverse pleasure from it. I could feel a heartbeat in my healing burns. My truck was not air-conditioned, a thing that wouldn't fly now, but then I drove with my arm out the window through the traffic of these desert towns. "I'm sorry. I didn't know. Should I go back? Over." I could see going back, surprising the girl. I wanted to see that girl again.

"It was on your sheet. Let it go this week. But let's read the sheet from now on. Over and out."

"Over and out," I said into the air, hanging up the handset.

Half the streets in Mesa were dirt, freshly bladed into the huge grid which now is paved wall to wall. I made several deliveries and ended up at the torn edge of the known world, the road just a track, a year maybe two at most from the first ripples of the growth which would swallow hundreds of miles of the desert. The house was an old block home gone to seed, the lawn dirt, the shrubs dead, the windows brown with dust and cobwebs. From the front yard I had a clear view of the Santan Mountains to the south. I was fairly sure I had a wrong address and that the property was abandoned. I knocked on the greasy door and after five minutes a stooped, red-haired old man answered. This was Gil, and I have no idea how old he was that summer, but it was as old as you get. Plus he was sick with the emphysema and liver disease. His skin, stretched tight and translucent on his gaunt body, was splattered with brown spots. On his hands several had been picked raw.

I didn't want to go into the house. This was the oddest call of my first day driving oxygen. There had been something regular about the rest of it, even the sanitized houses in Sun City, the upscale apartments in Scottsdale so new the paint hadn't dried, and the other houses I'd been to, magazines on a coffee table, a wife paying bills in the kitchen.

I pulled my dolly into the house, dark inside against the crushing daylight, and was hit by the roiling smell of dog hair and urine. I didn't kneel to wipe the wheels. "Right in here," the old man said, leading me back into the house toward a yellow light in the small kitchen, where I could hear a radio chattering.

He had his oxygen set up in the corner of the kitchen; it looked like he lived in the one room. There was a fur of fine red dust on everything, the range, the sink, except half the kitchen table where he had his things arranged, some brown vials of prescription medicine, two decks of cards, a pencil or two on a small pad, a warped issue of *Field & Stream,* a little red Bible, and a box of cough drops. In the middle of the table was a fancy painted plate, maybe a seascape, with a line of Oreos on it. I got busy changing out the tanks. You take the cardboard sleeve off, unhook the regulator, open the valve on the new tank for one second, blasting dust from the mouth, screw the regulator on it, open the pressure so it reads the same as you came, sleeve the old tank, load it up, and go. The new tank was always hot, too hot to touch from being in the sun, and it seemed wrong to leave such a hot thing in someone's bedroom. Nadine handled all the paperwork.

The cookies had scared me and I was trying to get out. Meanwhile the old man sat down at the kitchen table and started talking. "I'm Gil Benson," his speech began, "and I'm glad to see you, David. My lungs got burned in France in 1919 and it took them all these years to buckle." He spoke like so many of my customers in a hoarse whisper. "I've lived all over the world, including the three A's: Africa, Cairo, Australia, Burberry, and Alaska, Point Barrow. My favorite place was Montreal, Canada, because I was in love there and married the woman, had children. She's dead. My least favorite place is right here because of this. One of my closest friends was young Jack Kramer, the tennis player. That was many years ago. I've flown almost every plane made between the years 1938 and 1958. I don't fly anymore with all this." He indicated the oxygen equipment. "Sit down. Have a cookie."

I had my dolly ready. "I shouldn't, sir," I said. "I've got a schedule and better keep it."

"Grab that pitcher out of the fridge before you sit down. I made us some Kool-Aid. It's good."

I opened his refrigerator. Except for the Tupperware pitcher, it was empty. Nothing. I put the pitcher on the table. "I really have to go," I said. "I'll be late.

Gil lifted the container of Kool-Aid and raised it into a jittery hover above the two plastic glasses. There was going to be an accident. His hands were covered with purple scabs. I took the pitcher from him and filled the glasses.

"Sit down," he said. "I'm glad you're here, young fella." When I didn't move he said, "Really. Nadine said you were a good-looking kid." He smiled, and leaning on both hands, he sat hard into the kitchen chair. "This is your last stop today. Have a snack."

So began my visits with old Gil Benson. He was my last delivery every fourth day that summer, and as far as could tell, I was the only one to visit his wretched house. On one occasion I placed one of the Oreos he gave me on the corner of my chair as I left and it was right there next time when I returned. Our visits became little three-part dramas: my arrival and the bustle of intrusion; the snack and his monologue; his hysteria and weeping

The first time he reached for my wrist across the table as I was standing to get up, it scared me. Things had been going fine. He'd told me stories in an urgent voice, one story spilling into the other without a seam, because he didn't want me to interrupt. I had *I've got to go* all over my face, but he wouldn't read it. He spoke as if placing each word in the record, as if I were going to write it all down when I got home. It always started with a story of long ago, an airplane, a homemade repair, an emergency landing, a special cargo, an odd coincidence, each part told with pride, but his voice would gradually change, slide into a kind of whine as he began an escalating series of complaints about his doctors, the insurance, his children—naming each of the four and relating their indifference, petty greed, or cruelty. I nodded through all of this: I've got to go. He leaned forward and picked at the back of his hands. When he tired after forty minutes, I'd slide my chair back and he'd grab my wrist. By then I could understand his children pushing him away and moving out of state. I wanted out. But I'd stand—while he still held me—and say, "That's interesting. Save some of these cookies for next time." And then I'd move to the door, hurrying the dolly, but never fast enough to escape. Crying softly and carrying his little walker bottle of oxygen, he'd see me to the door and then out into the numbing heat to the big white pickup. He'd continue his monologue while I chained the old tank in the back and while I climbed in the cab and started the engine and then while I'd start to pull away. I cannot describe how despicable I felt doing that, gradually moving away from old Gil on that dirt lane, and when I hit the corner and turned west for the shop, I tromped it: forty-five, fifty, fifty-five, raising a thick red dust train along what would someday be Chandler Boulevard.

Backing up to the loading dock late on those days with a truck of empties, I was full of animal happiness. The sun was at its worst, blasting the sides of everything, and I moved with the measured deliberation the full day had given me. My shirt was crusted with salt, but I wasn't sweating anymore. When I bent to the metal fountain beside the dock, gulping the water, I could feel it bloom on my back and chest and come out along my hairline. Jesse or Victor would help me sort the cylinders and reload for tomorrow, or many days, everyone would be gone already except Gene, the swing man, who'd talk to me while I finished up. His comments were always about overtime, which I'd be getting if I saw him, and what was I going to do with all my money.

What I was doing was banking it all, except for pocket money and the eight dollars I spent every Sunday calling Linda Enright. I became tight and fit, my burns finally scabbed up so that by mid-July I looked like a young boxer, and I tried not to think about anything.

A terrible thing happened in my phone correspondence with Linda. We stopped fighting. We'd talk about her family; the cookie business was taking off, but her father wouldn't let her take the car. He was stingy. I told her about my deliveries, the heat. She was looking forward to getting the fall bulletin. Was I going to major in geology as I'd planned? As I listened to us talk, I stood and wondered: Who are these people? The other me wanted to interrupt, to ask: Hey, didn't we have sex? I mean, was that sexual intercourse? Isn't the world a little different for you now? But I chatted with her. Neither one of us mentioned other people, that is boys she might have met, and I didn't mention Elizabeth Rensdale. I shifted my feet in the baking phone booth and chatted. When the operator came on, I was crazy with Linda's indifference, but unable to say anything but "Take care, I'll call."

Meanwhile the summer assumed a regularity that was nothing but comfort. I drove my routes: hospitals Mondays, rest homes Tuesdays, residences the rest of the week. Sun City, Scottsdale, Mesa. Nights I'd stay up and watch the old movies, keeping a list of titles and great lines. It was as much of a life of the mind as I wanted. Then it would be six a.m. and I'd have Sun City, Scottsdale, Mesa. I was hard and brown and lost in the routine.

I was used to sitting with Gil Benson and hearing his stories, pocketing the Oreos secretly to throw them from the truck later; I was used to the new-carpet smell of all the little homes in Sun City, everything clean, quiet, and polite; I was used to Elizabeth Rensdale showing me her white breasts, posturing by the pool whenever she knew I was upstairs with her father. By the end of July I had three or four of her little moves memorized, the way she rolled on her back, the way she kneaded them with oil sitting with her long legs on each side of the lounge chair. Driving the valley those long summer days, each window of the truck a furnace, listening to "Paperback Writer" and "Last Train to Clarksville," I delivered oxygen to the paralyzed and dying, and I felt so alive and on edge at every moment that I could have burst. I liked the truck, hopping up unloading the hot cylinders at each address and then driving to the next stop. I knew what I was doing and wanted no more.

Rain broke the summer. The second week in August I woke to the first clouds in ninety days. They massed and thickened and by the time I left Sun City, it had begun, a crashing downpour. It never rains lightly in the desert. The wipers on the truck were shot with sun rot and I had to stop and charge a set at a Chevron station on the Black Canyon Freeway and then continue east toward Scottsdale, crawling along in the stunned traffic, water everywhere over the highway.

I didn't want to be late at the Rensdales'. I liked the way Elizabeth looked at me when she let me in, and I liked looking at her naked by the pool. It didn't occur to me that today would be any different until I pulled my dolly toward their door through the warm rain. I was wiping down the tank in the covered entry when she opened the door and disappeared back into the dark house. I was wet and coming into the air-conditioned house ran a chill along my sides. The blue light of the television pulsed against the darkness. When my eyes adjusted and I started backing up the stairway with the new cylinder, I saw Elizabeth sitting on the couch in the den, her knees together up under her chin, watching me. She was looking right at me. I'd never seen her like this, and she'd never looked at me before.

"This is the worst summer of my entire life," she said.

"Sorry," I said, coming down a step. "What'd you say?"

"David! Is that you?" Mr. Rensdale called from his room. His voice was a ghost. I liked him very much and it had become clear over the summer that he was not going back to Pennsylvania. He'd lost weight. His face had become even more angular and his eyes had sunken. "David."

Elizabeth Rensdale whispered across the room to me, "I don't want to be here." She closed her eyes and rocked her head. I stood the cylinder on the dolly and went over to her. I didn't like leaving it there on the carpet. It wasn't what I wanted to do. She was sitting in her underpants on the couch. "He's dying," she said to me.

"Oh," I said, trying to make it simply a place holder, let her know that I'd heard her. It was the wrong thing, but anything, even silence, would have been wrong. She put her face in her hands and lay over on the couch. I dropped to a knee and, putting my hand on her shoulder, I said, "What can I do?"

This was the secret side that I suspected from this summer. Elizabeth Rensdale put her hand on mine and turned her face to mine so slowly that I felt my heart drop a gear, grinding now heavily uphill in my chest. The rain was like a pressure on the roof.

Mr. Rensdale called my name again. Elizabeth's face on mine so close and open made it possible for me to move my hand around her back and pull her to me. It was like I knew what I was doing. I didn't take my eyes from hers when she rolled onto her back and guided me onto her. It was different in every way from what I had imagined. The dark room closed around us. Her mouth came to mine and stayed there. This wasn't education; this was need. And later, when I felt her hand on my bare ass, her heels rolling in the back of my knees, I knew it was the mirror of my cradling her in both my arms as we rocked along the edge of the couch, moving it finally halfway across the den as I pushed into her. I wish I could get this right here, but there is no chance. We stayed together for a moment afterward and my eyes opened and focused. She was still looking at me, holding me, and her look was simply serious. Her father called, "David?" from upstairs again, and I realized he must have been calling steadily. Still, we were slow to move. I stood without embarrassment and dressed, tucking my shirt in. That we were intent, that we were still rapt, made me confident in a way I'd never been. I grabbed the dolly and ascended the stairs.

Mr. Rensdale lay white and twisted in the bed. He looked the way the dying look, his face parched and sunken, the mouth a dry orifice, his eyes little spots of water. I saw him acknowledge me with a withering look, more power than you'd think could rise from such a body. I felt it a cruel scolding, and I moved in the room deliberate with shame, avoiding his eyes. The rain drummed against the window in waves. After I had changed out the tanks, I turned to him and said, "There you go."

He rolled his hand in a little flip toward the bedtable and his glass of water. His chalky mouth was in the shape of an O, and I could hear him breathing, a thin rasp. Who knows what happened in me then, because I stood in the little bedroom with Mr. Rensdale and then I just rolled the dolly and the expired tank out and down the stairs. I didn't go to him; I didn't hand him the glass of water. I burned; who would ever know what I had done?

When I opened the door downstairs on the world of rain, Elizabeth came out of the dark again, naked, to stand a foot or two away. I took her not speaking as just part of the intensity I felt and the way she stood with her arms easy at her sides was the way I felt when I'd been naked before her. We looked at each other for a moment; the rain was already at my head and the dolly and tank was between us in the narrow entry, and then something happened that sealed the way I feel about myself even today. She came up and we met beside the tank and there was no question about the way we went for each other what was going on. I pushed by the oxygen equipment and followed her onto the entry tile, then a moment later turning in adjustment so that she could climb me, get her bare back off the floor.

So the last month of that summer I began seeing Elizabeth Rensdale every day. My weekly visits to the Rensdale townhouse continued, but then I started driving out to Scottsdale nights. I told my parents I was at the library, because I wanted it to sound like a lie and have them know it was a lie. I came in after midnight; the library closed at nine. After work I'd shower and put on a clean shirt, something without my name on it, and I'd call back from the door, "Going to the library." And I knew they knew I was up to something. It was like I wanted them to challenge me, to have it out.

Elizabeth and I were hardy and focused lovers. I relished the way every night she'd meet my knock at the door and pull me into the room and then, having touched, we didn't stop. Knowing we had two hours, we used every minute of it and we became experts at each other. For me these nights were the first nights in my new life, I mean, I could tell then that there was no going back, that I had changed my life forever and I could not stop it. We never went out for a Coke, we never took a break for a glass of water, we rarely spoke. There was admiration and curiosity in my touch and affection and gratitude in hers or so I assumed, and I was pleased, even proud, at the time that there was so little need to speak. There was one time when I arrived a little early when Mr. Rensdale's nurse was still there and Elizabeth and I sat in the den watching television two feet apart on the couch, and even then we didn't speak. I forget what program was on, but Elizabeth asked me if it was okay, and I said fine and that was all we said while we waited for the nurse to leave.

On the way home with my arm out in the hot night, I drove like the young king of the desert. Looking into my car at a traffic light, other drivers could read it all on my face and the way I held my head cocked back. I was young those nights, but I was getting over it.

Meanwhile Gil Benson had begun clinging to me worse than ever and those prolonged visits were full of agony and desperation. As the Arizona monsoon season continued toward Labor Day, the rains played hell with his old red road, and many times I pulled up in the same tracks I'd left the week before. He stopped putting cookies out, which at first I took as a good sign, but then I realized that he now considered me so familiar that cookies weren't necessary. A kind of terror had inhabited him, and it was fed by the weather. Now most days I had to go west to cross the flooded Salt River at the old Mill Avenue Bridge to get to Mesa late and by the time I arrived, Gil would be on the porch, frantic. Not because of oxygen deprivation; he only needed to use the stuff nights. But I was his oxygen now, his only visitor, his only companion. I'd never had such a thing happen before and until it did I'd thought of myself as a compassionate person. I watched myself arrive at his terrible house and wheel the tank toward the door and I searched myself for compassion, the smallest shred of fellow feeling, kindness, affection, pity, but all I found was repulsion, impatience. I thought, surely I would be kind, but that was a joke, and I saw that compassion was a joke too along with fidelity and chastity and all the other notions I'd run over this summer. Words, I thought, big words. Give me the truck keys and a job to do, and the words can look out for themselves. I had no compassion for Gil Benson and that diminished over the summer. His scabby hands, the dried spittle in the ruined corners of his mouth, his crummy weeping in his stinking house. He always grabbed my wrist with both hands, and I shuffled back toward the truck. His voice, already a whisper, broke and he cried, his face a twisted ugliness which he wiped at with one hand while holding me with the other. I tried to nod and say, "You bet," and "That's too bad. I'll see you next week." But he wouldn't hear me any more than I was listening to him. His voice was so nakedly plaintive it embarrassed me. I wanted to push him down in the mud and weeds of his yard and drive away, but I never did that. What I finally did was worse.

The summer already felt nothing but old as Labor Day approached, the shadows in the afternoon gathering reach although the temperature was always 105. I could see it when I backed into the dock late every day, the banks of cylinders stark in the slanted sunlight, Victor and Jesse emerging from a world which was only black and white, sun and long shadow. The change gave me a feeling that I can only describe as anxiety. Birds flew overhead, three and four at a time, headed somewhere. There were huge banks of clouds in the sky every afternoon and after such a long season of blanched white heat, the shadows beside things seemed ominous. The cars and buildings and the massive tin roof of the loading dock were just things, but their shadows seemed like meanings. Summer, whatever it had meant, was ending. The fact that I would be going back to Montana and college in three weeks became tangible. It all felt complicated.

I sensed this all through a growing curtain of fatigue. The long hot days and the sharp extended nights with Elizabeth began to shave my energy. At first it took all the extra that I had being nineteen, and then I started to cut into the principal. I couldn't feel it mornings, which passed in a flurry, but afternoons, my back solid sweat against the seat of my truck, I felt it as a weight, my body going leaden as I drove the streets of Phoenix. Unloading became an absolute drag. I stopped jumping off the truck and started climbing down, stopped skipping up onto the dock, started walking, and every few minutes would put my hands on my waist and lean against something, the tailgate, the dock, a pillar.

"Oy, amigo," Jesse said one day late in August as I rested against the shipping desk in back of the dock. "Qué pasa?"

"Nothing but good things," I said. "How're you doing?"

He came closer and looked at my face, concerned. "You sick?"

"No, I'm great. Long day."

Victor appeared with the cargo sheet and handed me the clipboard to sign. He and Jesse exchanged glances. I looked up at them. Victor put his hand on my chin and let it drop. "Too much tail." He was speaking to Jesse. "He got the truck and for-got what I told him. Remember?" He turned to me. "Remem-ber? Watch what you're doing." Victor took the clipboard back and tapped it against his leg. "When the tanks start to fall, run the *other* way."

A moment later as I was getting ready to move the truck, Jesse came out with his white lunch bag and gave me his leftover burrito. It was as heavy as a book and I ate it like a lesson.

But it was a hot heedless summer and I showered every night like some animal born of it, heedless and hot, and I pulled a cot-ton T-shirt over my ribs, combed my wet hair back, and without a word to my parents, who were wary of me now it seemed, drove to Scottsdale and buried myself in Elizabeth Rensdale.

THE SUNDAY BEFORE Labor Day, I didn't call Linda Enright. This had been my custom all these many weeks and now I was breaking it. I rousted around the house, finally raking the yard, sweeping the garage, and washing all three of the cars, before rolling onto the couch in the den and watching some of the sad, throwaway television of a summer Sunday. In each minute of the day, Linda Enright, sitting in her father's home office, which she'd described to me on the telephone many times (we always talked about where we were; I told her about my phone booth, the heat, graffiti, and passing traffic), was in my mind. I saw her there in her green sweater by her father's rolltop. We always talked about what we were wearing and she always said the green sweater, saying it innocently as if wearing the sweater that I'd helped pull over her head that night in her dorm room was of little note, a coincidence, and not the most important thing that she'd say in the whole eight-dollar call, and I'd say just Levi's and a T-shirt, hoping she'd imagine the belt, the buckle, the trouble it could all be in the dark. I saw her sitting still in the afternoon shadow, maybe writing some notes in her calendar or reading, and right over there, the telephone. I lay there in my stocking feet knowing I could get up and hit the phone booth in less than ten minutes and make that phone ring, have her reach for it, but I didn't. I stared at the television screen as if this was some kind of work and I had to do it. It was the most vivid that Linda had appeared before me the entire summer. Green sweater in the study through the endless day. I let her sit there until the last sunlight rocked through the den, broke, and disappeared. I hated the television, the couch, my body which would not move. I finally got up sometime after nine and went to bed.

Elizabeth Rensdale and I kept at it. Over the Labor Day weekend, I stayed with her overnight and we worked and reworked ourselves long past satiation. She was ravenous and my appetite for her was relentless. That was how I felt it all: relentless. Moments after coming hard into her, I would begin to palm her bare hip as if dreaming and then still dreaming begin to mouth her ear and her hand would play over my genitals lightly and then move in dreamily sorting me around in the dark and we would shift to begin again. I woke from a brief nap sometime after four in the morning with Elizabeth across me, a leg between mine, her face in my neck, and I felt a heaviness in my arm as I slid it down her tight back that reminded me of what Victor had said. I was tired in a way I'd never known. My blood stilled and I could feel a pressure running in my head like sand, and still my hand descended in the dark. There was no stopping. Soon I felt her hand, as I had every night for a month, and we labored toward dawn.

In the morning, Sunday, I didn't go home, but drove way down by Ayr Oxygen Company to the Roadrunner, the truck

stop there on McDowell adjacent to the freeway. It was the first
day I'd ever been sore and I walked carefully to the coffee shop. I
sat alone at the counter, eating eggs and bacon and toast and coffee, feeling the night tick away in every sinew the way a car cools
after a long drive. It was an effort to breathe and at times I had
to stop and gulp some air, adjusting myself on the counter stool.
Around me it was only truck drivers who had driven all night
from Los Angeles, Sacramento, Albuquerque, Salt Lake City.
There was only one woman in the place, a large woman in a
white waitress dress who moved up and down the counter pouring coffee. When she poured mine, I looked up at her and our
eyes locked, I mean her head tipped and her face registered
something I'd never seen before. If I used such words I'd call it
horror, but I don't. My old heart bucked. I thought of my Professor Whisner and Western Civ; if it was what I was personally
doing, then it was in tough shape. The gravity of the moment
between the waitress and myself was such that I was certain to
my toenails I'd been seen: she knew all about me.

THAT WEEK I GAVE Nadine my notice, reminding her that I
would be leaving in ten days, mid-September, to go back to
school. "Well, sonnyboy, I hope we didn't work your wheels
off." She leaned back, letting me know there was more to say.

"No, ma'am. It's been a good summer."

"We think so too," she said. "Come by and I'll have your last
check cut early, so we don't have to mail it."

"Thanks, Nadine." I moved to the door; I had a full day of deliveries.

"Old Gil Benson is going to miss you, I think."

"I've met a lot of nice people," I said. I wanted to deflect this
and get going.

"No," she said, "you've been good to him; it's important. Some of these old guys don't have much to look forward to. He's called several times. I might as well tell you. Mr. Ayr heard about it and is writing you a little bonus."

I stepped back toward her. "What?"

"Congratulations." She smiled. "Drive carefully."

I walked slowly out to the truck. I cinched the chain hitches in the back of my Ford, securing the cylinders, climbed wearily down to the asphalt, which was already baking at half past eight, and pulled myself into the driver's seat. In the rearview mirror I could see Victor and Jesse standing in the shadows. I was tired.

Some of my customers knew I was leaving and made kind remarks or shook my hand or had their wife hand me an envelope with a twenty in it. I smiled and nodded gratefully and then turned businesslike to the dolly and left. These were strange goodbyes, because there was no question that we would ever see each other again. It had been a summer and I had been their oxygen guy. But there was more: I was young and they were ill. I stood in the bedroom doors in Sun City and said, "Take care," and I moved to the truck and felt something, but I couldn't even today tell you what it was. The people who didn't know, who said, "See you next week, David," I didn't correct them. I said, "See you," and I left their homes too. It all had me on edge.

The last day of my job in the summer of 1967, I drove to work under a cloud cover as thick as twilight in winter and still massing. It began to rain early and I made the quick decision to beat the Salt River flooding by hitting Mesa first and Scottsdale in the afternoon. I had known for a week that I did not want Gil Benson to be my last call for the summer, and this rain, steady but light, gave me the excuse I wanted. Of course, it was nuts to think I could get out to Mesa before the crossings were flooded. And by now, mid-September, all the drivers were wise to the monsoon and headed for the Tempe Bridge as soon as they saw overcast. The traffic was colossal, and I crept in a huge column of cars east across the river, noting it was twice as bad coming back, everyone trying to get to Phoenix for the day. My heart was only heavy, not fearful or nervous, as I edged forward. What I am saying is that I had time to think about it all, this summer, myself, and it was a powerful stew. The radio wouldn't finish a song, "Young Girl," by Gary Puckett and the Union Gap or "Cherish," by the Association without interrupting with a traffic bulletin about crossing the river.

I imagined it raining in the hills of Boulder, Colorado, Linda Enright selling cookies in her apron in a shop with curtains, a Victorian tearoom, ten years ahead of itself as it turned out, her sturdy face with no expression telling she wasn't a virgin any-more, and that now she had been for thirty days betrayed. I thought, and this is the truth, I thought for the first time of what I was going to say *last* to Elizabeth Rensdale. I tried to imagine it, and my imagination failed. I tried again, I mean, I really tried to picture us there in the entry of the Scottsdale townhouse speaking to each other, which we had never, ever done. When I climbed from her bed the nights I'd gone to her, it was just that, climbing out, dressing, and crossing to the door. She didn't get up. This wasn't *Casablanca* or *High Noon,* or *Captain Blood,* which I had seen this summer, this was getting laid in a hot summer desert town by your father's oxygen deliveryman. There was no way to make it anything else, and it was too late as I moved through Tempe toward Mesa and Gil Benson's outpost to make it anything else. We were not going to hold each other's faces in our hands and whisper; we were not going to stand speechless in the shadows. I was going to try to get her pants off one more time and let her see me. That was it. I shifted in my truck seat and drove.

Even driving slowly, I fishtailed through the red clay along Gil's road. The rain had moved in for the day, persistent and even, and the temperature stalled and hovered at about a hundred. I thought Gil would be pleased to see me so soon in the day, because he was always glad to see me, welcomed me, but I surprised him this last Friday knocking at the door for five full minutes before he unlocked the door, looking scared. Though I had told him I would eventually be going back to college, I hadn't told him this was my last day. I didn't want any this or that, just the little visit and the drive away. I wanted to get to Scottsdale.

Shaken up like he was, things went differently. There was no chatter right off the bat, no sitting down at the table. He just moved things out of the way as I wheeled the oxygen in and changed tanks. He stood to one side, leaning against the counter. When I finished, he made no move to keep me there, so I just kept going. I wondered for a moment if he knew who I was or if he was just waking up. At the front door, I said, "There you go, good luck, Gil." His name quickened him and he came after me with short steps in his slippers.

"Well, yes," he started as always, "I wouldn't need this stuff at all if I'd stayed out of the war." And he was off and cranking. But when I went outside, he followed me into the rain. "Of course, I was strong as a horse and came back and got right with it. I mean, there wasn't any sue-the-government then. We were happy to be home. I was happy." He went on, the rain pelting us both. His slippers were all muddy.

"You gotta go," I told him. "It's wet out here." His wet skin in the flat light looked raw, the spots on his forehead brown and liquid; under his eyes the skin was purple. I'd let him get too close to the truck and he'd grabbed the door handle.

"I wasn't sick a day in my life," he said. "Not as a kid, not in the army. Ask my wife. When this came on," he patted his chest, "it came on bang! Just like that and here I am. Somewhere." His eyes, which had been looking everywhere past me, found mine and took hold. "This place!" He pointed at his ruined house. "This place!" I put my hand on his on the door handle and I knew that I wasn't going to be able to pry it off without breaking it.

Then there was a hitch in the rain, a gust of wet wind, and hail began to rattle through the yard, bouncing up from the mud, bouncing off the truck and our heads. "Let me take you back inside," I said. "Quick, Gil, let's get out of this weather." The hail stepped up a notch, a million mothballs ringing every surface. Gil Benson pulled the truck door open, and with surprising dexterity, he stepped up into the vehicle, sitting on all my paperwork. He wasn't going to budge and I hated pleading with him. I wouldn't do it. Now the hail had tripled, quadrupled, in a crashfest off the hood. I looked at Gil, shrunken and purple in the darkness of the cab; he looked like the victim of a fire.

"Well, at least we're dry in here, right?" I said. "We'll give it a minute." And that's what it took, about sixty seconds for the hail to abate, and after a couple of heavy curtains of the rain ripped across the hood as if they'd been thrown from somewhere, the world went silent and we could hear only the patter of the last faint drops. "Gil," I said. "I'm late. Let's go in." I looked at him but he did not look at me. "I've got to go." He sat still, his eyes timid, frightened, smug. It was an expression you use when you want someone to hit you.

I started the truck, hoping that would scare him, but he did not move. His eyes were still floating and it looked like he was grinning, but it wasn't a grin. I crammed the truck into gear and began to fishtail along the road. I didn't care for that second if we went off the road; the wheels roared mud. At the corner, we slid in the wet clay across the street and stopped.

I kicked my door open and jumped down into the red mud and went around the front of the truck. When I opened his door, he did not turn or look at me, which was fine with me. I lifted Gil like a bride and he clutched me, his wet face against my face. I carried him to the weedy corner lot. He was light and bony like an old bird and I was strong and I felt strong, but I could tell this was an insult the old man didn't need. When I stood him there he would not let go, his hands clasped around my neck, and I peeled his hands apart carefully, easily, and I folded them back toward him so he wouldn't snag me again. "Goodbye, Gil," I said. He was an old wet man alone in the desert. He did not acknowledge me.

I ran to the truck and eased ahead for traction and when I had traction, I floored it, throwing mud behind me like a rocket.

By the time I lined up for the Tempe Bridge, the sky was torn with blue vents. The Salt River was nothing but muscle, a brown torrent four feet over the river-bottom roadway. The traffic was thick. I merged and merged again and finally funneled onto the bridge and across toward Scottsdale. A ten-mile rainbow had emerged over the McDowell Mountains.

I radioed Nadine that the rain had slowed me up and I wouldn't make it back before five.

"No problem, sonnyboy," she said. "I'll leave your checks on my desk. Have you been to Scottsdale yet? Over."

"Just now," I said. "I'll hit the Rensdales' and on in. Over."

"Sonnyboy," she said. "Just pick up there. Mr. Rensdale died yesterday. Remember the portable unit, okay? And good luck at school. Stop in if you're down for Christmas break. Over."

I waited a minute to over and out to Nadine while the news subsided in me. I was on Scottsdale Road at Camelback, where I turned right. That corner will always be that radio call. "Copy. Over," I said.

I just drove. Now the sky was ripped apart the way I've learned only a western sky can be, the glacial cloud cover broken and the shreds gathering against the Superstition Mountains, the blue air a color you don't see twice a summer in the desert, icy and clear, no dust or smoke. All the construction crews in Scottsdale had given it up and the bright lumber on the sites sat dripping in the afternoon sun. They had taken the day off from changing this place.

In front of the Rensdales' townhouse I felt odd going to the door with the empty dolly. I rang the bell, and after a moment Elizabeth appeared. She was barefoot in jeans and a T-shirt, and she just looked at me. "I'm sorry about your father," I said. "This is tough." She stared at me and I held the gaze. "I mean it. I'm sorry."

She drifted back into the house. It felt for the first time strange and cumbersome to be in the dark little townhouse. She had the air conditioning cranked way up so that I could feel the edge of a chill on my arms and neck as I pulled the dolly up the stairs to Mr. Rensdale's room. It had been taken apart a little bit, the bed stripped, our gear all standing in the corner. With Mr. Rensdale gone you could see what the room was, just a little box in the desert. Looking out the window over the pool and the two dozen tiled roofs before the edge of the Indian reservation and the sage and creosote bushes, it seemed clearly someplace to come and die. The mountains, now all rinsed by rain, were red and purple, a pretty lie.

"I'm going back Friday." Elizabeth had come into the room. "I guess I'll go back to school."

"Good," I said. "Good idea." I didn't know what I was saying. The space in my heart about returning to school was nothing but dread.

"They're going to bury him tomorrow." She sat on the bed. "Out here somewhere."

I started to say something about that, but she pointed at me. "Don't come. Just do what you do, but don't come to the funeral. You don't have to."

"I want to," I said. Her tone had hurt, made me mad.

"My mother and sister will be here tonight," she said.

"I want to," I said. I walked to the bed and put my hands on her shoulders.

"Don't."

I bent and looked into her face.

"Don't."

I went to pull her toward me to kiss her and she leaned away sharply. "Don't, David." But I followed her over onto the bed, and though she squirmed, tight as a knot, I held her beside me, adjusting her, drawing her back against me. We'd struggled in every manner, but not this. Her arms were tight cords and it took more strength than I'd ever used to pin them both against her chest while I opened my mouth on her neck and ran my other hand flat inside the front of her pants. I reached deep and she drew a sharp breath and stretched her legs out along mine, bumping at my ankles with her heels. Then she gave way and I knew I could let go of her arms. We lay still that way, nothing moving but my finger. She rocked her head back.

About a minute later she said, "What are you doing?"

"It's okay," I said.

Then she put her hand on my wrist, stopping it. "Don't," she said. "What are you doing?"

"Elizabeth," I said, kissing at her nape. "This is what we do. Don't you like it?"

She rose to an elbow and looked at me, her face rock-hard, unfamiliar. "This is what we do?" Our eyes were locked. "Is this what you came for?" She lay back and thumbed off her pants until she was naked from the waist down. "Is it?"

"Yes," I said. It was the truth and there was pleasure in saying it.

"Then go ahead. Here." She moved to the edge of the bed, a clear display. The moment had fused and I held her look and I felt seen. I felt known. I stood and undid my belt and went at her, the whole time neither of us changing expression, eyes open, though I studied her as I moved looking for a signal of the old ways, the pleasure, a lowered eyelid, the opening mouth, but none came. Her mouth was open but as a challenge to me, and her fists gripped the mattress but simply so she didn't give ground. She didn't move when I pulled away, just lay there looking at me. I remember it as the moment in this life when I was farthest from any of my feelings. I gathered the empty cylinder and the portable gear with the strangest thought: *It's going to take me twenty years to figure out who I am now.*

I could feel Elizabeth Rensdale's hatred, as I would feel it dozens of times a season for many years. It's a kind of dread for me that has become a rudder and kept me out of other troubles. That next year at school, I used it to treat Linda Enright correctly, as a gentleman, and keep my distance, though I came to know I was in love with her and had been all along. I had the chance to win her back and I did not take it. We worked together several times with the Democratic Student Alliance, and it is public record that our organization brought Robert Kennedy to the Houck Center on campus that March. Professor Whisner introduced him that night, and at the reception I shook Robert Kennedy's hand. It felt, for one beat, like Western Civilization.

THAT BAD DAY at the Rensdales' I descended the stair, carefully, not looking back, and I let myself out of the townhouse for the last time. The mud on the truck had dried in brown fans along the sides and rear. The late afternoon in Scottsdale had been scrubbed and hung out to dry, the air glassy and quick, the color of everything distinct, and the brown folds of the McDowell Mountains magnified and looming. It was fresh, the temperature had dropped twenty degrees, and the elongated shadows of the short new imported palms along the street printed themselves eerily in the wet lawns. Today those trees are as tall as those weird shadows. I just wanted to close this whole show down.

But as I drove through Scottsdale, block by block, west toward Camelback Mountain, I was torn by a nagging thought of Gil Benson. I shouldn't have left him out there. At a dead end by the Indian School canal I stopped and turned off the truck. The grapefruit grove there was being bladed under. Summer was over; I was supposed to be happy.

Back at Ayr Oxygen, I told Gene, the swing man, to forget it and I unloaded the truck myself. It was the one good hour of that day, one hour of straight work, lifting and rolling my empties into the ranks at the far end of the old structure. Victor and Jesse would find them tomorrow. They would be the last gas cylinders I would ever handle. I locked the truck and walked to the office in my worn-out workshoes. I found two envelopes on Nadine's desk: my check and the bonus check. It was two hundred and fifty dollars. I put them in my pocket and left my keys, pulling the door locked behind me.

I left for my junior year of college at Missoula three days later. The evening before my flight, my parents took me to dinner at a steakhouse on a mesa, a western place where they cut your tie off if you wear one. The barn-plank walls were covered with the clipped ends of ties. It was a good dinner, hearty, the baked potatoes big as melons and the charred edges of the steaks dropping off the plates. My parents were giddy, ebullient, because their business plans which had so consumed them were looking good. Every loan they'd positioned was ready; the world was right. They were proud of me, they said, working hard like this all summer away from my friends. I was changing, they said, and they could tell it was for the better.

After dinner we went back to the house and had a drink on the back terrace, which was a new thing in our lives. I didn't drink very much and I had never had a drink with my parents. My father made a toast to my success at school and then my mother made a toast to my success at school and to my success with Linda Enright, and she smiled at me, a little friendly joke, and she clinked her scotch and water against my bottle of Bud and tossed it back. "I'm serious," she said. Then she stood and threw her glass out back and we heard it shatter against the stucco wall. A moment later she hugged me and she and my father went in to bed.

I cupped my car keys and went outside. I drove the dark streets. The radio played a steady rotation of exactly the same songs heard today on every fifty-thousand-watt station in this country; every fifth song was the Supremes. I knew where I was going. Beyond the bright rough edge of the lights of Mesa I drove until the pavement ended, and then I dropped onto the red clay roads and found Gil Benson's house. It was as dark as some final place, and there was no disturbance in the dust on the front walk or in the network of spiderwebs inside the broken storm door. I knocked and called for minutes. Out back, I kicked through the debris and weeds until I found one of the back bedroom windows unlocked and I slid it open and climbed inside. In the stale heat, I knew immediately that the house was abandoned. I called Gil's name and picked my way carefully to the hall. The lights did not work, and in the kitchen when I opened the fridge, the light was out and the humid stench hit me and I closed the door. I wasn't scared, but I was something else. Standing in that dark room where I had palmed old Oreos all summer long, I now had proof, hard proof, that I had lost Gil Benson. He hadn't made it back and I couldn't wish him back.

Outside, the cooked air filled my lungs and the bright dish of Phoenix glittered to the west. I drove toward it carefully. Nothing had cooled down. In every direction the desert was being torn up, and I let the raw night rip through the open car window. At home my suitcases were packed. Some big thing was closing down in me; I'd spent the summer as someone else, someone I knew I didn't care for and I would be glad when he left town. We would see each other from time to time, but I also knew he was no friend of mine. I eased along the empty roadways trying simply to gather what was left, to think, but it was like trying to fold a big blanket alone. I kept having to start over.